DATE DUE

MR 1 8 '92			
NO 4 '92			
	261-2500		Printed in USA

CLOVER

CLOVER

♣ ♣ ♣

A Novel by Dori Sanders

G.K.HALL&CO.
Boston, Massachusetts
1990

© 1990 by Dori Sanders.

Published in Large Print by arrangement with
Algonquin Books of Chapel Hill,
a division of Workman Publishing Company, Inc.

G.K. Hall Large Print Book Series.

Set in 18 pt. Plantin.

Library of Congress Cataloging-in-Publication Data

Sanders, Dori, 1934–
    Clover : a novel / Dori Sanders.
      p. cm.—(G.K. Hall large print book series)
    Summary: After her father dies within hours of being married to a
white woman, a ten-year-old black girl learns with her new mother to
overcome grief and to adjust to a new place in their rural black
South Carolina community.
    ISBN 0-8161-5048-6
    1. Large type books.   [1. Afro-Americans— Fiction.
2. Interracial marriage—Fiction. 3. Large type books.] I. Title.
[PZ7.S1977C1 1990b]
[Fic]—dc20
                                                   90-38994

*To my family
for their patience and humor
and
To Nancy Shulman
who saw in me something
I did not see in myself*

One

♣ ♣ ♣

They dressed me in white for my daddy's funeral. White from my head to my toes. I had the black skirt I bought at the six-dollar store all laid out to wear. I'd even pulled the black grosgrain bows off my black patent leather shoes to wear in my hair. But they won't let me wear black.

I know deep down in my heart you're supposed to wear black to a funeral. I guess the reason my stepmother is not totally dressed in black is because she just plain doesn't know any better.

The sounds inside our house are hushed. A baby lets out a sharp birdlike cry. "Hush, hush, little baby," someone whispers, "don't you cry." There is the faint breathless purr of an electric fan plugged in to help out the air-conditioning, the hum of the refrigerator going on in the kitchen, a house filled

1

with mourners giving up happy talk for the quiet noise of sorrow.

We take the silence outside to waiting shiny black cars, quietly lined behind a shiny black hearse. Drivers in worn black suits, shiny from wear, move and speak quietly, their voices barely above a whisper. It seems they are afraid they might wake the sleeping dead. It's like the winds have even been invited. The winds are still.

One of the neighbors, Miss Katie, is standing in the front yard, watching the blue light on top of a county police car flash round and round. She is shaking her head and fanning the hot air with her hand. Biting, chewing, and swallowing dry, empty air. Her lips folding close like sunflowers at sundown—opening, like morning glories at dawn.

They asked Miss Katie to stay at the house. Folks in Round Hill, South Carolina, never go to someone's funeral and not leave somebody in their home. They say the poor departed soul just might have to come back for something or another, and you wouldn't want to lock them out.

My breath is steaming up the window of the family car. It's really cold inside. Someone walks to our driver and whispers something.

2

I see a cousin rush from a car with what Grandpa would have called a passel of chaps. They leave our front door wide open. A hummingbird flies to the open door and stands still in midair, trying to decide about entering, but quickly darts backward and away.

I press my face against the cold window. Only a few days back, my daddy, Gaten, walked out that very door, carrying a book. He headed toward the two big oak trees in the front yard and settled himself into the hammock that was stretched between them. And after awhile, like always, he was sound asleep, with the open book face down across his chest.

My daddy looked small between those big trees. But then, he was small. Everybody says I'm small for a ten-year-old. I guess I'm going to be like my daddy. Funny, it's only the middle of the week, but it seems like it's Sunday.

They say I haven't shed a single tear since my daddy died. Not even when the doctor told me he was dead. I was just a scared, dry-eyed little girl gazing into the eyes of a doctor unable to hold back his own tears. I stood there, they said, humming some sad

3

little tune. I don't remember all of that, but I sure do remember why I was down at the county hospital.

Things sure can happen fast. Just two days before yesterday, my aunt Everleen and I walked in and out of that door, too. Hurrying and trying to get everything in tip-top shape for Gaten's wedding supper.

Gaten didn't give Everleen much time. He just drove up with this woman, Sara Kate, just like he did the first time I met her. Then up and said flat-out, "Sara Kate and I are going to get married. She is going to be your new stepmother, Clover."

I almost burst out crying. I held it in, though. Gaten couldn't stand a crybaby. "A new stepmother," I thought, "like I had an old one." I guess Gaten had rubbed out his memory of my real mother like he would a wrong answer with a pencil eraser.

Everleen had been cooking at her house and our house all day long. My cousin Daniel and I have been running back and forth carrying stuff. I should have known something was up on account of all the new stuff we'd gotten. New curtains and dinette set for the kitchen. Everleen said, "The chair seats are covered in real patent-leather." Gaten's room was really pretty. New rug and bed-spread with matching drapes.

In spite of all the hard work Everleen was doing, she had so much anger all tied up inside her it was pitiful. She was slinging pots and pans all over the place. I didn't know why she thought the newlyweds would want to eat all that stuff she was cooking in the first place. Everybody knows that people in love can't eat nothing.

Even Jim Ed tried to tell her she was over-doing it. "It didn't make any sense," her husband said, "to cook so much you had to use two kitchens."

"I don't want the woman to say I wouldn't feed her," Everleen pouted.

"I think Sara Kate is the woman's name, Everleen," Jim Ed snapped.

Well, that set Everleen off like a lit fire-cracker. She planted her feet wide apart, like she was getting ready to fight. Beads of sweat poured down her back. The kitchen was so hot, it was hard to breathe.

Jim Ed gave his wife a hard look. "I hope you heard what I said."

Everleen put her hands on her hips and started shaking them from side to side so fast, she looked like she was cranking up to takeoff. "I heard what you said, Jim Ed.

5

Heard you loud and clear. What I want to know is, what you signifying?"

Everleen was so mad, she looked like she was going to have a stroke. "Let me tell you one thing. Get this through your thick skull and get it straight. You are not going to get in your head that just because some fancy woman is marrying into this family you can start talking down to me. You better pray to the Lord that you never, and I mean never, embarrass me in front of that woman. Because if you do, only the Lord will be able to help you." She waved a heavy soup spoon in his face. "Another thing, Jim Ed Hill, I am not going to burn myself to a crisp in that hot peach orchard getting my skin all rough and tore up. I'm sure all Miss Uppity-class will do is sit around, and play tennis or golf. One thing is the Lord's truth, she is not going to live off what our . . ." She stopped short. "I mean what your folks worked so hard to get. Everleen Boyd will not take anything off anybody no matter what color they may be. I've been in this family for a good many years, but I sure don't have to stay."

My uncle looked at me. I guess he could see I was hurting. He put his arm around me. "Oh, baby, we ought to be ashamed, carrying on like this. We can't run Gaten's life for him. And we sure don't need to go out of our way to hurt him. Gaten told me out of his own mouth, he truly loves the woman he's going to marry. My brother deserves some happiness. You are going to have to help him, also, Clover. Getting a stepmother will be something new for you to get used to."

Jim Ed turned to his wife. "You always say you put everything in the Lord's hands. I think you better put this there, too, and leave it there, Everleen." Well, that quieted Everleen down. She never bucks too much on advice about the Lord.

Right then I couldn't even think about the stepmother bit. All I could think about was what Everleen said. Maybe she was thinking of leaving Jim Ed and getting a divorce. She called herself Boyd. I didn't think she wanted to be a Hill anymore. If she took her son Daniel and left me all alone with that strange woman, I would die. I knew in my heart, I would surely die.

I was starting to not like my daddy very much. Not very much at all. Miss Katie says, "Women around Round Hill leave their husbands at the drop of a hat these days." If

Everleen leaves it will all be Gaten's fault, I thought. All because of his marriage plans.

Everleen pulled me from Jim Ed to her side. I buried my face against her sweaty arm, glad there was the sweat so she couldn't feel the tears streaming down my face. Her hot, sweaty smell, coated with Avon talcum powder, filled my nose. It was her own special smell. I felt safe.

Finally she pushed me away. "Let me dry them tears," she said, dabbing at my eyes with the corner of her apron. I should have known, I couldn't fool her.

I don't know if it was what Jim Ed said about Gaten or the Lord that turned Everleen around. Probably what he said about the Lord, but it sure turned her around. After a few minutes she was her old self again.

"All right, little honey," she said, "we better get a move on. We got us a marriage feast to cook. Now I'm going to put together the best wedding supper that's ever been cooked. Then I'm going to dress you up in the prettiest dress your daddy has ever laid eyes on." She glanced at my hair. "Lord have mercy, Allie Nell's still got your hair to fix."

Anyway, Everleen was still cooking and

cleaning at the same time when the telephone rang. My daddy had been in a bad accident. Everleen snatched lemon meringue pies out of the oven and drove her pickup like crazy down to the hospital.

The sign in the waiting room said "NO SMOKING," but Uncle Jim Ed smoked anyway. He let long filter-tipped paper jobs dangle from his mouth and almost burn his lips before he remembered to take a draw.

There was an intercom system like the one at school. A voice was repeating, "Code blue—code blue. Room number 192." Nurses from everywhere hurried down the long hall.

Everleen stirred her hand around inside her pocketbook like she was stirring a pot of boiling grits. She pulled out a handful of candy without a piece of paper on it and divided it between me and Daniel. Daniel ate his. I didn't eat mine. I can't stand candy from Everleen's pocketbooks. It's the same as sucking down perfume.

It was getting later and later, and I still hadn't seen my daddy. The sun was setting. It had cast its last shadows for the day. Those long, lean shadows, they crept through the windows and clung to the clean hall floors, waiting for the darkness to swallow them up.

A state highway patrolman appeared in the doorway of the waiting room. He inched forward slowly—it seemed as if he was afraid to enter the room. He turned his hat around and around in his hands. My uncle Jim Ed knew him. He had gone to high school with my daddy.

"I was called to the scene of the accident," he finally said.

Aunt Everleen didn't make it easy for the state trooper to tell us what had happened. Her body was shaking and drawing up like she was having spasms. Although she held Jim Ed's big white handkerchief all balled up in her fist, she did not use it. Most likely because he had blown his nose into it before he handed it to her. I guess with all that was going on, poor Jim Ed plumb forgot what he was doing.

So Everleen sat there, working her mouth back and forth to hold it back from screaming out loud. Tears flowed from her eyes too full to hold them any longer. They ran down her face and formed tiny streams around her neck, that was already dripping wet with sweat.

"Tell us what happened," she would

plead. Then in the next breath, cry out, "No, no, no. I don't want to hear. I can't bear knowing." Then she'd turn right around and beg once again for him to tell her what happened.

The state trooper finally refused to listen any longer. With his hat still in his hand, he turned his back and said, "Gaten Hill's car was struck by a pickup truck when the driver ran a signal light at the intersection of North Main Street and Highway 74. Police at the scene said alcohol is believed to have contributed to the accident which is under investigation."

He shook his head. "The car was struck on the driver's side. Gaten was driving. It looks bad," he said, "real bad." The state trooper started shaking his head again.

I thought to myself, if the wreck was all that bad, perhaps my daddy needed me. As soon as he left, I sneaked from the waiting room.

It was suppertime. I could smell the food. My daddy is always hungry for supper. I've always helped get his supper. Something seemed to tell me he needs me. I have to find him. When no one was looking I slipped down the long hall.

When a nurse popped out of a room, I hid

11

behind a tall stack of covered trays. The nurse stopped and faced the blank wall, for a long time, studying the blank wall, looking at it as though it was some kind of picture, as though she was trying to make out a face or something. Wide fancy framed eyeglasses dangled from a chain around her neck.

I peeped from behind the trays with the little round tins covering the plates, like an Easter bonnet pulled down too far on a child's head.

While the big fat nurse with the eyeglasses studied the blank wall, I studied her shoes. White crepe-soled shoes with heels run-over so far, the shoe touched the floor. She didn't even see me when she took one of the trays from the cart.

A big set of doors swung wide open. Two doctors dressed in rumpled green started down the hall.

"This is the absolute worst part of it all," one of them said.

The other doctor loosened the mask that covered everything on his face except his eyes, "I understand there is a child. A little girl."

"At least she has one of them."

"I'll talk with the family now."

I hope they don't mean something bad has

happened to Sara Kate, I thought. Gaten will be so sad. I waited until they were out of sight and hurried back to the waiting room to hear what they were going to say about Sara Kate.

A nurse led me into a small office. The doctor was speaking in a soft, soft voice, yet it was strong and heavy with sadness. Uncle Jim Ed and Everleen were carrying on like the world was coming to an end. Then I knew something was wrong. Bad wrong. A nurse offered little white pills in thimble-sized plastic cups to Aunt Everleen and Uncle Jim Ed.

Aunt Everleen buried her face in her hands and covered her ears with her fingers when the doctor tried to explain how Gaten died. For her, it was enough that he was dead.

But Uncle Jim Ed leaned forward in his chair and listened. He listened and cried. Aunt Everleen's face showed she heard the sad-faced doctor explain that my daddy's internal injuries were too extensive for them to save him.

The doctor put his hand on my shoulder. "I want to see my daddy," I said. "I need to see him." But he wouldn't take me to see Gaten. His blue eyes filled with tears. He turned away, "I'm sorry," he whispered. "We couldn't save your father."

The doctor wouldn't let me see my daddy, but he took me to Sara Kate's room to see her. The state trooper sure had been right. Sara Kate was some kind of bad bruised and cut up. Her eyes were closed. Maybe, like her lips, they were swollen shut.

The doctor's voice was soft, like our footsteps had been. Soft like snowflakes falling on the ground. "Mrs. Hill, Mrs. Hill," he repeated until she had slowly opened her eyes. Maybe she was so slow about it because she hadn't gotten used to her new name. After all, she had only had it for a few hours.

She smiled a quick weak half-smile and closed her eyes again. I guess there wasn't much for her to keep them open to see. Just a doctor in a rumpled green cotton outfit and me. I still hadn't gotten my hair fixed and, like always, I had sort of messed up my tee shirt a little scraping the bowl in which Aunt Everleen made the lemon butter creme icing for her fresh coconut lemon layer cake. Plus, with Daniel not around, I got to lick the ice cream dasher.

Sara Kate bit her swollen lip. And even on a face that messed-up, sadness found itself a place. "Oh, little Clover," she whispered.

The doctor gave me a "say something" look.

"Hey," I said, "I'm very pleased to see you, ma'am." Then I pulled loose from the doctor's light grip on my hand and backed out of the room.

All I had heard my daddy say about her meant absolutely nothing to me. I still did not know the woman. To me she was a total stranger. How could I know her? It takes time to learn a person.

My aunt wanted to pray for me. With me. I didn't feel like praying. It seemed like all the praying I'd done hadn't helped anyway, not one single bit. While I was hiding behind those trays, I prayed for my daddy not to die. I'd prayed for my grandpa, too. Even prayed for my mama to come back to me. I just can't pray no more. It won't do me any good no way.

It's strange, but as soon as Gaten died it seems everybody sort of knew he was going to die. They could all remember some little thing he'd said, something strange about the way he was acting. They all could see some change. From the way everybody's talking, it seems Gaten visited every living soul in Round Hill, South Carolina.

All I can think is, if all those people knew something was going to happen to Gaten, wonder why they didn't do something to stop it from happening?

Some people claimed they didn't even know it was going to be Gaten. They just knew something terrible was going to happen to someone. Somebody's left eye jumped. A black cat crossed the road to the left, in front of another person's car. When that happens something bad is bound to follow.

Uncle Jim Ed doesn't seem troubled in the least that people keep coming up and saying all those kind of things. He simply said, quietly, "There is something so awesome about death, baby girl, people feel compelled to address it in some way. I suppose it's to make some peace with themselves to answer the last unknown."

With a silent owl-like swoop, the cars pulled into line and away. Car engines purring like an arrangement of music. Notes written for a sad song.

At the end of a row of rosebushes, a broken rose dangled down on one of the bushes.

Broken, because I tried to break it off to pin on my dress but couldn't. You wear a white rose if your mother is dead. I don't know what color you wear when your daddy dies. I guess it probably doesn't matter.

Miss Katie is waving a big white handkerchief. They didn't tell Sara Kate that Miss Katie was left behind with the food just in case some stranger might come by, hungry and in need of a place to rest awhile. Just by chance it might be the departed soul. They only told Sara Kate it was an old custom, handed down through many generations. They did tell her, though, that the reason the hands on all clocks in the house had been stopped at 6:45 P.M. was because that was when Gaten died. People coming in only had to ask if it was morning or evening.

The only time Sara Kate said anything about the funeral arrangements was when they wanted to bring Gaten's body home and have the wake there. They said he should spend his last night on earth at home. "Oh no, oh no," Sara Kate whispered. "I don't think I can handle that." She did let them bring him by the house in the hearse the day of the funeral.

Sara Kate is sitting next to my daddy's

only brother, Uncle Jim Ed. Her eyes are closed. She is twisting her new wedding band on her finger. Sara Kate is not old, but she is making the sounds with her mouth that old people make when they are beside themselves and don't know which-a-way to turn. Quiet, dry-lipped, smacking sounds. Lips slowly opening and closing, smack, smack. Just like Miss Katie.

A group of small barefoot children stand on the side of the blazing hot, hard-surfaced road. So thin, they look like stick figures. Big wide eyes pop out from faces like big white cotton balls on a blackboard. They turn and walk backwards, waving their sticklike arms until the long line of cars are out of sight. I wave back.

Sara Kate is standing alone before Gaten's casket. Her husband. My father. The funeral crowd has been held back. She has her own private time. Just a little stretch of time to be alone with Gaten. Small silent moments to say goodbye to someone already lost to her forever. All eyes are upon her. She is a white woman, a stranger to Round Hill.

Sara Kate is looking down at Gaten. Gaten's necktie is crooked. His necktie was always crooked. There was that strange connection between them that I could never understand. At least twice that I can remember, there had been a quick look from Sara Kate, and Gaten would give her a slight smile and straighten his necktie. And then smile a smile for her alone. Now Sara Kate looked at Gaten, but Gaten did not straighten his necktie.

I guess that strange and curious connection between them is gone forever.

As far as looks go, Gaten had a look for me, too. There was a certain look between us, but it sure was not the same kind of look he and Sara Kate had. For me, Gaten's look did almost everything. Most of the time he didn't have to question or punish me. His look did it all.

There was one look my daddy gave me that I don't think I'll ever forget as long as I live. It happened the day my teacher, Miss Wilson, marched me down to his office. All the years I'd gone to Gaten's school, I'd never been in any kind of trouble, much less something bad enough to be sent to the principal's office. Gaten had enough trouble at school without me adding to it.

I think my teacher hated to take me a whole lot worse than I hated to go. "Bringing

Clover here, sir, was my very last resort."
My daddy took off his eyeglasses. "Please
don't apologize, Miss Wilson. Clover is
my daughter, but she is also one of your
students. I would have been disappointed in
you as a teacher if you had treated her dif-
ferently because of me. I'll keep Clover here
with me for the rest of the day."

After Miss Wilson left I inched up to Gaten's desk. "I'm sorry, Daddy," I said. "I
didn't mean to cause trouble. Honestly I
didn't."

Gaten sucked in his breath. I could tell he
hated for me to call him daddy at school.
Calling him daddy caused a change in his
feelings toward me. It showed. A two-year-
old could see that. Besides, when a daddy is
all you have left, you end up with double
love. At least that's the way it was until Miss
Sara Kate came along.

Anyway, as I was saying, Gaten looked
away from me. "Get a pencil and paper, Clover, and write down everything you want to
tell me that happened in your classroom this
afternoon." Then my daddy looked at me.
It was such a disappointed look, I could
barely keep from crying.

"Maybe you'd rather tell me, Clover," he
said. I studied the floor, swaying from side

to side, shifting my feet one over the other. "No sir," I said. I never raised my head. No computer for me today, I can see. So I balanced my notebook on my knees and wrote. Gaten said, "Write everything you *want* to tell me that happened."

I didn't *want* to tell him nothing that really happened. How do you tell your daddy you showed off so you wouldn't have to take a test? A test you knew in your heart that you could never get a passing grade on.

When they started this thing of testing in the schools, I sure hate it that I made such a high score on that old IQ test. Made everybody think I'm so-oo smart. But I know I'm not. I've always been good in math. My grandpa taught me figures and stuff before he taught me to read. He said, "The most important thing a person needs to know is how to hold on to their money." There's no way for me not to be good in spelling. My uncle Jim Ed's wife, Aunt Everleen, has had my head buried in a dictionary since I was in the third grade. She wants me to make it to that Washington, D.C., spelling bee so bad she can taste it.

And poor old Gaten, he still thinks I'm a genius because he believes I learned to drive a tractor just by him telling me what to do.

To this day he still doesn't know Grandpa taught me to drive a tractor as soon as I turned eight. He made me promise not to tell my daddy until I was older. My grandpa died that same year.

I just sort of guessed at most of the other stuff on the test. Like, I figured "ruth" would mean the opposite of "cruelty" since Grandpa said she was a good woman from the Bible. Gaten said most people knew "ruthless," but never even thought of "ruth" as a word. I didn't tell him I never did, either.

All of this was really Gaten's fault. Looks like he should have known in the first place I couldn't have learned to drive a tractor that quick, just because he told me what to do.

I was playing at the edge of our backyard when I heard a moaning sound. At first I thought it was the old stray hound having another litter of pups. And I sure didn't want to see that. Not again. Then I heard a weak cry for help and raced to the tractor shed. There was Gaten. His leg was pinned between the tractor wheel and spray machine. He had been hooking up the machine to spray peaches when the tractor probably slipped out of gear and rolled back.

Gaten's voice was getting weak. He was bleeding like a butchered hog. "Get Jim Ed," he whispered.

I started to cry. "Uncle Jim Ed went to get a load of fertilizer."

I grabbed my daddy to try and pull him out, but he made me stop. "This tractor has got to be moved," he groaned and closed his eyes.

"I can do it, Gaten," I cried. "I can, I can. Please let me."

"You can't even reach the clutch, Clover."

"I can if I stand up."

"You don't know how to change gears."

"Yes I do," I almost said, but said instead, "I will if you tell me how to do it."

Gaten thought I was some kind of genius when I pulled that tractor off him.

Grandpa said that once I've learned something I'm like an old cooter, it's hard for me to turn it loose. I guess he thought comparing me to an old green turtle was a compliment. But what's got me worried now is, there's bound to be all new stuff in this new test. Stuff I've never heard of in my entire life. Just because I'm good at spelling and know the meaning of a whole bunch of words in the dictionary is not enough. Everything you need to know is not in there.

23

I tap my foot on the carpeted floor, like I'm bouncing a ball. Thump, thump. Gaten looks up. "Did you finish your report, Clover?" I shake my head, no. "Don't shake your head, Clover, say yes or no, Mr. . . ." Gaten breaks off. He never, ever made me call him mister. I giggle out loud.

There is no way I could tell Gaten why I was brought to his office. So I wrote and wrote.

I can't get away with stuff like I can when I'm waiting in Gaten's office to go home after school. I ride the school bus in the morning. Gaten has to leave before Aunt Everleen has time to fix my hair. I'm the only girl in the fifth grade who doesn't fix her own hair. Gaten says it looks too bushy when I do it.

Once I almost got away with sharpening a whole stack of pencils to a nub on his new electric pencil sharpener. Gaten didn't fuss or nothing. Just said, "I think you've sharpened enough pencils, Clover, do your homework." I do believe Gaten will be telling me to do my homework for the rest of my life. Then there was the time he told me to wear a dress on picture-taking day, and I slipped and wore my rust corduroy skirt. It was bad twisted but still pretty. When Gaten saw it, all he said was, "Straighten your skirt, Clover."

But this time it was different. My daddy was really upset with me. He didn't say much, but I could tell.

When I gave Gaten my written report, there was a trace of a smile on his face when he read it. There was real laughter in his eyes. But it was gone when he looked at me. His mouth tightened. "A bald eagle flying through an open window to attack a snake curled in a striking position behind Miss Wilson's desk?" Gaten's voice was strong. "Come now, Clover, are you trying to tell me this happened in the classroom?"

"Shucks no, Gaten," I said. "That's what I was thinking about when Miss Wilson asked me to read my history report."

The school janitor opened Gaten's office door and jumped backwards, "Excuse, excuse me, sir," he says over and over. "I didn't aim to come in with you in here."

Gaten glanced at his watch and stood up. "It's getting late, Mr. Jackson, we'll get out of your way."

I made a grin at Gaten's back. Hot dog, Aunt Everleen will have our dinner on the stove, all warm and everything. Gaten will read while I stand on the little stool he made for me and fix his plate. If he kept on making me write everything I've ever learned in my whole life, I wouldn't have time to fix his ole plate.

The janitor was so glad Gaten called him mister. He grinned and squinted his pink eyes. Mr. Jackson is an albino. He stood tall and straight and grinned over that "mister" bit. Gaten was old enough to be his father.

People are still filing past my daddy's coffin. Sara Kate is wedged between me and Uncle Jim Ed, squeezed in between us on the crowded bench like vanilla cream between dark chocolate cookies. My daddy is dead. Stretched out in a fancy coffin right before my very eyes. And all I can think of is an Oreo cookie. An Oreo cookie.

My stepmother's body is as straight as a cornstalk. She is not crying. We sit side by side as stiff as painted leaves on a painted tree. Uncle Jim Ed puts his hand on her arm. But me and my stepmother don't touch. I can count on the fingers of one hand how many times I've laid eyes on Sara Kate. She's been my stepmother for almost four days and all I know for sure about her is, she's not a Mexican. I can spot a Mexican a mile away. Every summer if there's a big peach crop the migrant workers flood Round Hill. We have peaches, but not enough to need the Mexicans.

Chase Porter brings them in all the time. He couldn't get all those peaches picked without them. He's one of the biggest peach growers in South Carolina. Chase is at the funeral. He looks sad because he is sad. He has known my daddy all his life. Like Gaten he was born and raised in Round Hill.

I pick at a thorn in my finger until it starts to bleed. I watch a drop of blood threaten to fall. I turn my finger into a paint brush. The blood makes a round dot on my white dress. I keep adding to it until it almost becomes a flower. A daisy. The way I'm messing up my white dress, I might as well have held the baby with the stinky diaper. At first there had been just one little drop of blood that a bleeding finger could not leave alone. My dress is a mess. Sara Kate reaches for my hand. I put it behind my back.

In a way the funeral was kind of like a play. Everyone had a part. A part they played right on time, like it had been rehearsed over and over until it was down pat.

An usher leads me to my daddy's coffin. I'm supposed to cover my daddy's face with the white satin quilted blanket. He is dead. Yet he still looks some kind of fine in that fancy casket. But my arms are pasted to my sides. My knees glued together. There is no way I can pull that thing over Gaten's face. They lead me away. My feet slide across the floor like it's a sheet of ice. It's a sad, sad thing to have a ten-year-old do.

A young woman takes a picture of Gaten in the coffin. I don't think Sara Kate liked that much, either. Her face shows her feelings straight out.

The men in black suits move quickly and quietly about the casket. They close the casket. Lock the brass handles into place. It's time for the funeral to start. The Ninetieth Psalm is read. I guess my daddy is like the green grass only he was cut down before he could wither and fade. A young student sings. When a boy sings, he sings so much sadder than a girl. Everybody from the county sheriff on down is crying. Everybody but Sara Kate and me.

The women in white dresses that have stood waiting in line take the flowers off Gaten's casket and follow as he is carried away. At the graveyard they finish their part in the play. The curtain has been dropped. It's the end.

Sara Kate places a single rose on Gaten's coffin. Gaten had been put away real fine.

A group of men in dirty coveralls and dirty shovels walked toward the grave with long smooth steps like the gliding wings of buzzards flying down to feast on the dead.

If there was a hungry stranger who stopped while we were away, he didn't eat nothing. There is still food piled up everywhere. And he didn't move or take anything either. My teddy bears are in the same place. Their eyes still have the same fixed blank stares. The snow-filled paperweight is still on Gaten's desk, right beside his new solar calculator. I shake the paperweight. A heavy snowfall twirls around, then gently settles down on a tiny village. Soon all is quiet and peaceful. The tiny snow-covered village is asleep. Not a picture is missing from the crowded piano top. Not a single piece of carnival glass moved.

Even outside everything is the same. Nothing has been changed. A soft breeze gently sways the hammock sometimes. But mostly the hammock is still. Still and empty, like it's waiting.

If there was a stranger there, one thing is for sure. He did not disturb or take away the heavy sadness in the house. Every bit of that was left behind, right in place.

The house is soon filled with people from top to bottom. The kitchen is filled with women fixing plates. Someone brings Sara Kate a plate. She moves the food around with a fork but she doesn't eat a bit. I can understand that. I can't eat anything, either.

A mother pulls her little four-year-old boy in the middle of the room to sing. He's going to sing, just to take our minds off so much sadness, she says. He sings "America the Beautiful." He keeps his head to one side, his eyes on the floor. He sings pretty good, but how can anyone think someone would want to hear that song when their daddy is dead? But the little boy in the blue suit and red-checkered bowtie sways like he is in a swing, and sings and sings. In the end he hides his face behind his hand. He is not too shy to eat, though.

I was so sure Sara Kate was going to leave Round Hill and go back wherever she came from. I started packing my clothes to move out. I wasn't sure who I was going to live with. I only knew I was not staying in that house by myself.

I'm going to learn someday that whenever

my uncle Jim Ed and his sister gather in a little cluster with Sara Kate, they're bound to be talking about me. Yes, it is me they're talking about. Sometimes Aunt Ruby Helen's voice really gets loud. She is looking cross-eyed at Sara Kate. "It will be best for my dead brother's child to be with me," she says. "I am her daddy's only sister. Actually, the only family the poor child has." Uncle Jim Ed is not about to let his sister get away with that. "Clover still has me," he says quietly. "I'm family, and she's used to us."

His sister's voice is loud again. This is the first time she's been able to even talk. She lost her voice as soon as she got off the plane. She's been crying ever since. Tears streaming down her face like rain. Her mouth was crying, but there were no crying sounds. Her brother's death took away her voice, just like death took away his life. Just sucked it up.

"You have a child, Jim Ed, a son. I have no one. Besides, Clover needs a mother." Like a child, Ruby Helen is pleading with her brother.

I guess she would make a pretty good mother. I got me a Cabbage Patch doll from her, way before anybody else in Round Hill got one. I guess Maryland is not the worst place in the world to live. If I go there I bet

I'll start walking like Ruby Helen. I know she copied making short, swishing steps from Jackée on the TV program "227."

One wants me to stay, one wants me to leave. I guess they will have to do like the old wise king Grandpa told me about. Just cut me in half.

A tight-lipped Sara Kate says, "I promised Clover's father I would take care of his daughter." In her own quiet way, Sara Kate sure said the right thing to Settle that. Nobody around here messes with a dying man's wishes.

Ruby Helen looks at the corner cupboard Grandpa built with all of Grandmother's carnival glass. "My grandmother won every single piece of that glass at the county fair shooting down ducks. It is very, very valuable," she said coldly to Sara Kate.

I can see Jim Ed is embarrassed. "I'm sure Sara Kate will see that nothing is broken," he tells his sister. I'm thinking first, that was some kind of a cold thing to say to Sara Kate and second, I'd thought all along it had been *my* grandmother, Ruby Helen's mother, who did all that straight shooting.

Two

♣ ♣ ♣

It shouldn't have surprised me that Sara
Kate and I would end up together, because
she was a surprise for me from the start. She
sure wasn't a purple bicycle.

"I thought I told you I was bringing a
surprise home, honey. Aunt Everleen didn't
get a dress ready for you," my daddy whispered. He was looking at my torn dirty dress.

I pulled on my dress, my eyes on his shiny
loafers. I could tell Gaten had put a lot into
making everything right for this surprise.
But when he rolled up with that woman in
his truck and no purple bicycle, the surprise
thing was over for me.

"Everleen had a whole bunch of dresses
washed," I shot back hotly, "but she just
ironed this one. She claimed she was having
hot flashes so bad, they were about to set
her on fire. I can see her getting hot in the
summertime, but she's been hot all winter.

"You may not believe this, Gaten," I went

33

on, "but Everleen's been running as hot as an overheated radiator all winter. One day she was standing on the front porch fanning like it was the Fourth of July, and there was snow on the ground. Cross my heart and hope me die, she was."

I could see I'd hurt Gaten bad. Real, real bad. It showed in his eyes.

"I didn't know I was going to mess around and fall trying to catch that old lightning bug, Gaten," I said all sorry-like.

Now that I think about it, Everleen must have known something I didn't. She did my hair pretty and dressed me up really fine. Gaten always did have this thing about hair. He wanted my hair to look just right.

The only thing I knew was, Gaten was going to bring me a surprise and I'd been waiting all day long for it. In the back of my mind I imagined it would be a ten-speed purple bicycle. Every wish I ever made, I wanted a bicycle. Surely Gaten must have known that.

I knew it wouldn't be another doll. Ever since I cut open the high-priced one Gaten got me to see what made her cry, he hadn't bought me another one. He wasn't really that mad, though. He just looked over his glasses at me and said, "I think my little girl will become a fine surgeon one day."

He sure wouldn't have gotten me a cat or dog. Maybe he's scared I might cut them up or something. I really don't care, though. We got more strays around now than you can shake a stick at.

The trouble was, I had to wait too long for Gaten to come. It was starting to get dark. The trees had started to show up against the evening sky like a picture under thin tracing paper. It made a pretty picture. Trees drawn in black ink on a sky framed with soft gray and pink clouds. Tiny gnats bunched together in small groups to dance their daily yo-yo dance at dusk.

When lightning bugs started darting through the sky, I jumped to catch one and landed smack dab in a pile of rotting watermelon rinds. How was I to know that's where Jim Ed threw them when we finished eating? I got me some pretty diamond rings, though.

I still wouldn't have gotten as dirty as I did if I hadn't seen the little raised furrow an old mole was making in the ground. It almost made my flesh crawl to see that dirt cracking open, like a train going through a tunnel. It kind of like drives me crazy to see dirt moving, and you can't see what's making it move. I've never, ever been able to find a mole. One day, I guess, I'll just dig my fool head clean off.

So, you see, I got some kind of dirty, waiting on Gaten all that time.

This woman, Sara Kate, is going to take some getting used to. We didn't set horses from the start. When I showed Gaten the diamond rings I made, she shivered and eyed me coldly. "Oh, how cruel," she said, catching her breath all short and quick, like she was hurting or something. "So cruel," she whispered, when I answered, "Yes, I killed the lightning bugs." I don't know how in the world she thought I got the stuff to make my rings.

Gaten didn't say a word. He knew better than to open his mouth because he taught me how to make the rings in the first place. I guess he did it, though, to stop me from running myself to death over the dew-filled grass.

You see, on bright, sunshine-filled days, if there's been a heavy dew, the light makes diamonds everywhere. When I was little I used to race to pick up one, only to have it disappear right before my eyes. Everleen told Gaten to make me stop before I went storm crazy. Besides, she said, the sores on my legs would never heal if I kept getting dew in them.

Gaten never said a word about the dew diamonds. I just quit on my own. Just like I stopped looking for the pot of gold Grandpa said was at the end of the rainbow. I still like the lightning bug diamonds, thought. To me, they look kind of real.

Sara Kate can't seem to get her mind off the fireflies, as she calls them. If she's gonna stick around us, she sure better get used to things being killed. Gaten would shoot anything that flies, except a dove. My grandpa always said, "Never kill a dove because unaware you might kill a messenger."

My daddy told me to change my dress so we could go to the fish camp for supper.

"There is no way I'm going to the fish camp to eat," I said. "For all I know they might catch them fish in the creek. Mr. Saye Willie Adams said he wouldn't eat no fish at the fish camp if he was on his dying bed and the fish would save him." I turned to Sara Kate, "And you wouldn't either if you knew what the boys in Round Hill do in the creek water."

When Gaten tried to excuse what I'd said to Sara Kate, and make me apologize for making up what awful thing, I didn't back down. I said, "All I know is what they say, and that's exactly what they say. Besides, Gaten," I added, "we have supper anyhow. I heated up the stew we had last night, and Everleen sent over a fresh pot of rice."

I knew Gaten was still plenty mad at me over this creek thing. But then I was a little mad at him, too. To this day I can't see how Gaten could think that his bringing a woman I'd never laid eyes on in my life could possibly be a surprise for me. Especially a woman that might become my stepmother. Even if I got a purple bike, I didn't want a step-mother. Even if I had to have one, I sure wouldn't pick one like Sara Kate.

Looks like anybody who knows the story about Cinderella should know that nobody in the world would want a stepmother unless they were all the way crazy.

For days on end Gaten had been walking around in a daze. He looked like he was about to die or something. Jim Ed said he'd been bitten by the love bug. In my head I think he was still mad about that creek water thing. And just maybe he knew I slipped and read that letter Sara Kate wrote him. I hate like everything I read that letter. That's the first time I'd ever read Gaten's mail in my life. But it was too late then. I couldn't unread what I'd read. Even if Gaten knew I read the thing, he surely couldn't think that I could begin to understand that letter.

My dearest Gaten,
    Now that I'm faced with this dreadful thought of losing you, I'm not sure what direction my life will take. I only know that it seems necessary to convey to you how deeply I care about you. I know, as you do, that happiness cannot be built upon the pain of others. And yet, your sensitivity to this only serves to add to my reasons for loving you.
    My faith is in your wisdom and my trust in your decision.
Always,
Sara Kate

I can't see why Sara Kate couldn't just say straight out what she's trying to tell my daddy. But whatever it is, I guess he must have made some sense out of it. He's mighty disturbed over something.

Everybody knew something was bad wrong with Gaten when he wouldn't eat. At Sunday's dinner Gaten didn't eat chicken or rib one. Wouldn't even eat a spoonful of Everleen's banana pudding. I could have eaten the whole thing by myself. She puts Cool Whip on top instead of that egg white stuff. They said Gaten was in L.O.V.E.

I wish I hadn't read his old letter. If I hadn't, then I wouldn't have known he'd lost her.

It was a black night outside, and Gaten was staring out the window. His eyes searched through the darkness. I wondered if he thought his Sara Kate might just come through the darkness back to him.

Three

♣ ♣ ♣

Everyone at the family gathering was solid
blown away when Gaten strolled up with
Miss Sara Kate. Everybody, that is, except
Gideon. He didn't even look up. He just kept
right on eating away on a long slice of watermelon and spitting out seeds.

At least we all knew why it took Gaten so
long to get back with the salt for the ice
cream churn. He had been all the way to the
airport in Charlotte, North Carolina.

In a way I didn't mind too much that Sara
Kate was there. Maybe Gaten would get his
mind settled down and his appetite back.

The relatives of our family were all gathered at our house. They've done that every
year for as long as I can remember.

All the old folks pulled chairs under a
shade tree. They made their way around
with shaking unsteady steps, like they were
picking their way barefoot through broken
glass. They settled their bodies, thin from

age, down among walkers and walking sticks, their voices as weak as their eyes tucked into wrinkled faces that pulled together like a gathered skirt. In the summer's heat they gathered together like sparrows warming themselves in the winter sun. Old age sure makes up its own gathering.

Deep down in my heart I knew before that day was over Sara Kate was going to be sick, sick. I could tell from the look on her face when she saw that boiling grease in that big black iron washpot. She had never seen fish cooked like that in her life. Still, whenever someone brought her a piece she ate it. Just like she ate Aunt Ruby Helen's peach walnut cake, then turned right around and ate a big hunk of store-bought Sunbeam Spanish Bar. The cake tastes all right if you can get past that awful gooey white icing that's as thick as the cake. And that's not counting the biscuits. Every time my great uncle stabs one with a fork for him, he stabs one for Sara Kate and puts it on her plate.

It seems at least the yellow jackets like the Sunbeam cake icing. I tell Sara Kate to be careful of the yellow jackets. If they sting her it might make her swell up like Uncle Jim Ed does when he gets stung. He's allergic to bees.

Poor old Sara Kate didn't even turn down the ham Gideon cooked, even after everybody tried to warn her it came from a boar. But then, the woman doesn't even know what mountain oysters are. I knew. I'd known for a long time. But I sure knew better than to tell her. You see, it's a right nasty thing to repeat.

Gaten sure needed to stay by her side. Annie Ruth, another umpteen cousin, piled macaroni and cheese on Sara Kate's plate. Annie Ruth looked plain country. Her hair was in tight separate curls all over her head. She won't comb her hair, she explained, because she is trying to save her beauty shop hairdo until Sunday. "I'm getting so worried about my mind here of late," she complained. "I get ready to use it, and Lord it's plumb left me. Sometimes I can't find it for days."

Gaten could have helped Sara Kate out on Aunt Maude's potato salad. Everyone knows she is as clean as a whistle even if she can't half see. But who wants to crunch through eggshells and spit out pieces of onion skin? But then, Gaten was eating it, too. I guess he hated to see everybody turning her potato salad down. Gaten is tender-hearted.

Sara Kate's eyes shifted from Annie

Ruth's hair to yet another cousin. Her eyes were glued on the little girl's head. Her mama had her hair all corn-rowed up in the tiniest rows I'd ever seen. Rows going backwards, forwards, and all across the head. Like a cornfield planted by a drunk driving the tractor. I imagined Sara Kate was trying to count all the rows. If she wasn't, she had to be studying the haircuts. Some of the cousins, including Daniel, had razor parts cut so crazy across their heads it looked like a lightning bolt was zigzagging across.

To top all that off, our cousin California came in with even more corn-rows on her head. Her corn-rows were set in like a patchwork quilt. California is off in the head. So are her parents. They are constantly on the move all the time, moving toward and away from each other, like the checkers move about a checkerboard. Moves that form a retarded dance.

My little cousin with the corn-rows stands beside California, her eyes and head cast downward, her fat arms folded across her wide fat body.

Maybe I don't like their corn-rows because I know I can never wear them. Aunt Everleen said she'd rather be struck by a bolt of lightning than to corn-row my hair. I won't sit still long enough. Perhaps, in a way, I might be a little bit jealous.

California heads straight to a banana pudding. You better not mess around with her, though. Once Daniel was mocking the way she held her mouth open with spit drooling down. And he told her if she kept it that way they would send her back to the asylum in Columbia, South Carolina. Yes, California has been in the asylum.

Well, anyway, California got so mad she tried to ram Daniel's head into a rusty tin gallon can. I don't know what they did to her down there, but it seems like she came back worse off than she was.

Daniel knew it was wrong to mock her in the first place. Grandpa told us that long ago in Bible times the Lord sent down two bears to kill up a bunch of kids because they mocked one of his prophets.

California is taking a liking to Sara Kate. She seems drawn to her hair and keeps touching it. I know one thing, she better not let my daddy's sister from Maryland catch her combing Sara Kate's hair. Up there, Ruby Helen claims they made the people in some town change a picture of a little black girl combing a white woman's hair while they watched a polo game.

I can't name all that food on the tables. Gaten pushes Miss Eula Mae's wheelchair out of the sun into a shady spot. I go over and fan away the old nasty blow-fly buzzing around her food. When she finishes I see a dollar bill she has for me, in fingers bent over like a curved fork. Gaten is watching so I don't take it. But when he looks away that dollar is in my hands like a flash.

There was one thing I could tell right off. There was hardly a woman there who could stand Sara Kate. From a corner at the top of the stairs I can see in the dining room, but they can't see me. A cousin draws on a cigarette and slowly releases the smoke through her nose.

Ruby Helen laughs long, and hard. "I haven't seen anybody do that since old man Dan Rivers died."

"Girl, you remember some old-timey stuff."

"Remember how he used to roll his cigarettes and wet 'em with so much spit they split open?"

Their voices were drowned out by their loud laughter. I couldn't imagine Sara Kate laughing like that. All I'd heard her do that day was giggle.

Everleen comes in with a pot of soup. "I'm starting to bring in stuff," she said. "Somebody go scrape out that ice cream in the churn and put it in the freezer. Poor old Gaten will want some later. He loves homemade cream. Bless his heart, he was too shamed to eat from the dasher like he always used to. His fancy lady friend sure cramps his style."

"Seems like your brother-in-law is going to bring home a lady," someone says.

"Gaten won't marry again."

"You don't have to marry a lady to bring her home."

Everleen pulls her mouth into a tight ugly spout. "Gaten Hill does."

The cousin is dipping a homemade white potato roll into the soup. Smacking and licking her thick red lips. Everleen's jaw tightens. "Get a bowl, girl. Stop eating nasty in my soup."

They are talking about Sara Kate again.

"Can't you just die from all that beige and taupe she's wearing?"

"Girl, them some Gloria Vanderbilt's pants."

"Aw shucks now, go on, girl."

"Wonder what's wrong with her?"

"I don't know, but there is something

47

that's caused her to be rejected by her own men."

"I say she's an epileptic," Ruby Helen puts in. The cousin puts a small slice of egg custard pie in her mouth, all at once. "How in the Lord's world did you come up with that affliction, Ruby Helen?"

"I can't stand it when someone talks with a mouth full of food."

The cousin swallowed hard. "So tell me, how do you know?"

"It's the way her eyes get that blank stare. You can be talking to her, but she's not there."

"She could be in a deep study about something."

"Well, something's wrong with her. Why else would she take up with a black dude?"

In spite of how hard they try to put down my daddy's new woman friend, trying to make her have some kind of sickness is bad. Next they will say she is retarded.

I really think it's her background that has upset them, and made them so jealous and hopping mad. You can look at the woman and see she is certainly not poor trash. Uncle Jim Ed told me she is an only child and would never starve if she didn't hit a lick at work for the rest of her life. Not that it makes him like her any better. He hasn't made up his mind that she is the right woman for his baby brother.

He can't find fault with the way she seems to care about Gaten. Nobody can. Not over the way she looks at him. Her eyes follow his every move. She wears her feelings for him right on her face. I sure can see why she likes him. My daddy is pretty cool-looking. He is not light-skinned, but he's not dark-skinned, either. Since he cut off his mustache you can see his mouth and nose better. He's got a great mouth, especially when he smiles. And I don't care if he is a man, his nose is plain pretty. It's good Sara Kate is too old to grow anymore. Right now she and Gaten are the same height. And that's not real tall. My aunt says my daddy could stand to put on a few pounds.

I like the way they are together. They are not all over each other, hugging and kissing like some courting people. Every now and again she touches him when he is near, her hand lightly touching his, or an elbow resting on his knee.

Someone brings the cousin's little baby inside. "Well," the cousin says, dabbing spit on the tips of her fingers and wiping dried milk from around her baby's mouth, "this Sara Kate must have what Gaten likes."

"Oh, gross, Mary Kathyrn," Ruby Helen moaned. "I do hope you never let Gaten's high-class Miss Sara Kate see you do that. She'll think all black women wash their kids faces with spit."

"Sh-sh," someone whispered, "here comes Merlee Kenyon. Poor little thing. She is sure taking it hard since she and Gaten broke up. I don't know why she didn't leave when Gaten drove up with his new lady friend."

Ruby Helen eyed Merlee's tight white pants, red, red blouse and high-heeled red sandals. "Girl, you are looking bad, bad."

Miss Kenyon did look good that day, and she's got a bad shape. The prettiest shape I ever saw.

My aunt let Merlee know right off that she could not stand Sara Kate. Merlee and my aunt always were close friends.

I couldn't help thinking that it was half-way my aunt's fault that Gaten ended up with Sara Kate in the first place.

Not long after my daddy broke off with Miss Kenyon, he said he needed to get away for awhile. So he had my aunt Everleen get me all fixed up and we took off to Maryland for a long weekend.

It had been my aunt's idea to go see the King Tut exhibition. Once we got there and saw the long lines, she changed her mind. We were getting ready to leave when she spotted one of her neighbors, a doctor at Howard University Hospital, waiting in line.

While they chatted, the doctor's beeper went off. I thought that was some kind of cool. I wished my daddy had one. Gaten volunteered to hold his place in line while he made his phone call.

It turned out he was on call at the hospital and had to leave. Gaten said the position in line was too good to give up. So he stayed. My aunt and I went shopping.

At breakfast the next morning, Gaten said he couldn't believe that just by chance he had bumped into someone he hadn't seen in years. "I mean I literally bumped into her," he laughed. "When I turned to apologize, we recognized each other. We first met during my last year in college."

Ruby Helen looked at me. "So that's the reason your daddy called to say he wouldn't be home for supper. I don't think he would have missed supper if he had known I'd baked a capon and made wild rice dressing."

I sure didn't see what had been so special about the meal. Just another chicken dinner, as far as I was concerned.

"Well," she said to Gaten, "maybe I'll see more of you up here now. It's said that it takes some woman to force a man to visit his people."

"The woman you've mentioned doesn't live in this area," Gaten said quietly. "In fact," he continued, "because of her work with the textile industry, she might temporarily move to the Carolinas. She's a textile designer."

Gaten poured syrup over his pancakes. He smiled at his sister. "Pure Vermont maple syrup. At least someone in the Hill family knows how to live."

If there is anything my aunt knows, it's food. Her husband travels in his work all the time. She stays home and eats. My aunt is as big as a house. She is still kind of pretty, though.

"Just wait until you sink your teeth into the fried cornmeal mush I'm going to cook," she promised Gaten. "Remember how Mama used to let the cooked mush set overnight in the cold on the back porch so it would slice good the next morning? We would drench those crisp golden brown fried slices with fresh butter and molasses. But you haven't tasted anything until you've had it with pure maple syrup."

Gaten laughed. "We only had it if it was cold weather. Mama never realized the refrigerator would have done the same job. She had to do it the way her mama did."

It was so good between the two of them, remembering the times when they were young. If only it had ended there. But Ruby Helen had to keep on running her mouth and jump back on the lady he had dinner with.

I had no idea what my aunt meant when she said to my daddy, "Well, there is certainly nothing wrong with a one-night stand. At least it didn't used to be, but these days," she paused and raised her eyebrows, "a decent family man sort of stays away from that kind of thing." She piled more pancakes on my plate. "If you catch my drift, big brother."

I didn't know what she meant then. I still don't know. But what I did know was, I didn't believe anyone had ever made Gaten so mad before. He put his knife and fork on his plate. In the right position, of course. Gaten eats very proper. He learned all that stuff in college. "Thanks for breakfast, Sis," he said.

If my daddy hadn't been so mad I believe he would have broken down and flat out cried.

I suppose whatever that one-night stand business was about, my aunt shouldn't have said it, or at least not in front of me. Anyway, I know that was what caused Gaten to end up cutting our visit a little short. Again, I didn't get a chance to see the White House.

"It's amazing," Miss Kenyon said, "how one single turn in your life will lead you down a road of no return. How one, single unintentional act can affect you for the rest of your life."

Miss Kenyon looked at Ruby Helen. "I don't know why you would let your brother get all tied up with a woman like her in the first place. Gaten should have sense enough to know that kind of a marriage never works out."

My aunt shrugged. "Who says he is going to marry her?"

"You know full well he will." Miss Kenyon's voice is sharp and cutting. "And you and Jim Ed will stand by with your hands folded and let it happen."

Ruby Helen squeezed her eyes into narrow slits. "Merlee Kenyon, tell me you are not accusing me of getting my brother and that white woman together. I may look like I'm crazy, sound like I'm crazy, but listen up, honey, and listen good, I am nobody's fool."

Miss Kenyon dropped her head. "I'm sorry, Ruby Helen. So very sorry. I'm not blaming you. There is really no one to blame but myself. Me and my big mouth."

She moved to the curtained dining room windows, and stood peeking out at Gaten and Sara Kate.

A group of women dug through mounds of filled green plastic trash bags, carefully examining rolled and wadded paper napkins. Poking with sticks through chicken and rib bones. They were searching for Cousin Amphia's false teeth, of course. Every year she takes them out to eat, wraps them in a paper napkin and they get lost every time.

Amphia appears to be lost too. Wandering around worrying over her teeth. Her bright red toenails stick out of her open-toed sandals. Her toenails look as if she painted them with a spray can.

Miss Kenyon looked so lonely and sad I felt sorry for her. I knew she was crying inside. My aunt must have known it, too.

She excused herself and left the room for awhile.

When Merlee moved to Round Hill from Greenville, South Carolina, everybody said she was without a doubt the prettiest black woman they had ever seen. Merlee thought so, too. And she didn't try to hide it.

I know she was the best piano player I ever heard. I also knew she almost drove my poor daddy crazy. He couldn't keep his mind on nothing.

They were really tight for awhile. Nobody had to tell me about it. I knew it for a fact. Her car was parked at our house so much, Aunt Everleen warned her she'd better slack off some, people would start to talk.

And then some talk started. Talk got out that Miss Kenyon said she was in love with Gaten Hill, all right and enough, but she wasn't about to take on a ready-made family. She also said she sure didn't spend the best years of her life getting a master's degree in music to take care of someone else's child. Besides, little girls get on her nerves, she added.

As soon as I heard what she had said I made up my mind that I was not about to show her the killdeer's nest I'd seen. I had found a good hiding place in a tree near the edge of a field and watched the little chirping bird build the nest right on the ground. It seemed the little killdeer found the smoothest little round rocks and gravel. It rolled them into a pile with its bill, then settled down on top of the little rounded-out nest like a setting hen.

I was supposed to have started taking music lessons from Miss Kenyon every Saturday morning. I had planned to take her to see the killdeer's nest when we finished the lesson. But I didn't even start taking the old piano lessons. I didn't care what Gaten would have said. I didn't show her my bird nest, either. That was for sure.

Well, when Gaten heard what his girlfriend said about me, he stopped courting her altogether.

I kind of thought Gaten might have said something about the music lessons. But he didn't. He didn't say anything about Miss Kenyon, either.

Once when I was waiting in his office for him to finish working, I said, "Gaten, we didn't really need Miss Kenyon, did we? We can get along real good without anyone, can't we?"

Gaten leaned back in his chair and smiled

at me, "Real good, Clover," he said, "real good." When my daddy smiled, he was the best-looking man in the whole world.

I don't know if it was what Merlee Kenyon said about not liking little girls, or what she said about my mama, that hurt Gaten so much. "I really don't want to wear a dead woman's shoes," she'd said, adding that even the woman's backwoods furniture made her almost throw up. She also said she could hardly keep from throwing out all the tacky little whatnots my mother left in the house.

According to Miss Katie, "A woman should never, ever talk about a man's dead wife. They may not have gotten along worth a hoot when married. But if and when a woman dies, she suddenly becomes a saint in her husband's eyes."

Downstairs the dining room filled up with women again.

"Gaten's new lady seems to like his little Clover a lot," someone said to Miss Kenyon.

The truth is, Miss Sara Kate was singing a different tune from the first time I met her. I overheard her say to my daddy, "Clover is indeed a beautiful little girl, Gaten, You must love her dearly."

"Yes," Gaten smiled, "she is quite beautiful, and yes, I do love that little girl." He laughed. "She is also difficult sometimes, and as you well know, one can never tell what's going to come out of her mouth."

Sara Kate had laughed, a rich husky laugh that seemed strange coming from someone with a childish voice. "Tell me about it," she said.

I couldn't help but think, this woman's got the smarts to say the right thing at the right time. She may not have wanted me any more than Miss Kenyon wanted me. People don't like to take on extras. But just maybe, I figured, she had sense enough not to say it. At least not to someone who would carry it back to Gaten.

Yes, I'd decided, Sara Kate could so fool Gaten if she really wanted to. Poor old Gaten, he just might be simple-minded enough to believe that if Sara Kate would be happy with Clover, then Clover would be happy with her.

Everleen brings a platter piled high with fried chicken. "There's enough food left over to feed an army. Where's Clover? Her daddy is looking for her."

"Probably at the top of the stairs listening," laughs Ruby Helen.

I sneak out of a dormer window and, when no one is looking, slide down the chinaberry tree at the end of the porch. I need to find my daddy anyway. I got some kind of a bad stomachache and it looks like I'm not the only one.

Aunt Everleen could certainly tell something was wrong with Sara Kate. "Go find out if there is anything I can do for her, Clover," she said.

"Leave them alone," Cousin Lucille said. "When people are in love they want to be alone. Alone behind closed doors."

If anybody had looked at Sara Kate right good, they would have known by the way she looked, the way she walked, weakly leaning on Gaten. She certainly was not leaving for any hanky-panky, like they said.

Gaten and Sara Kate were in his bedroom. They were alone all right. But the door sure wasn't closed. It was wide open. Sara Kate was lying on the bed, her head propped up on a pillow. Gaten sat on the bed by her side, trying to get her not to talk. But Sara Kate talked anyway. She kept saying over and over, "I'm so sorry, Gaten, so very sorry. Why did I have to get sick?"

"It's because you've been eating like a crazy person," I said. I brought her a foaming glass of Alka-Seltzer, and put a cold damp face cloth on her forehead. My daddy hugged me, and said, "Brilliant." It wasn't anything. I've done the same thing a thousand times for Aunt Everleen when she gets one of her migraine headaches.

People are starting to leave. Sara Kate is sitting all alone at the end of a long table. What little lipstick she had on is all gone. She is as white as a sheet. She looks as sick as a dog.

A dying day brings on dying moods. A cousin up from lowlands is playing his guitar and singing the blues. "Lord, Lord," he sings, "sometimes I feel like I'm dying." He kind of looks like he's dying, with his red eyes and puffy lips that look like somebody put purple lipgloss on them.

Gideon's beagle hounds are raising some kind of fuss. Running some poor little rabbit, as hot as it is.

"Pick that thing, baby," Cousin Lucille says to the guitar player. She has put herself together as carefully as a clown. She is wearing every shade of purple I believe there is. I'm surprised her hair isn't purple. She is wearing a new wig, a frizzed one. The old one caught on fire while she was bending over a gas burner.

Lucille must have forgotten she's supposed to be a born-again Christian now and given up dancing. Because now she can't hold her dancing spirit down. Either that or it's those chiggers setting her body on fire. She's been in the blackberry thickets every day.

Somebody said, "She looks like she's having a spell the way she's twisting and carrying on."

"Leave her alone," Ruby Helen said. "She lost her husband." By that she meant, not lost like you can't find him. Everybody in Round Hill knows where he is. Right in the cemetery under an old stunted pine tree. He's dead.

So Lucille danced, all alone in the still twilight. A lonely woman whose body wins out over a guilty heart. I don't care if Lucille's getup was unlike anything you'd ever seen. It still made all the menfolk look at her. And that made the womenfolk kind of jealous. I think it's because of her walk, not her dancing. Lucille's walk is a swaying motion, her soft, curvy hips move under her skirt. I wouldn't mind having her shape when I grow up.

It's too bad Lottie Jean has gone home with the new camera she got with her S&H green stamps. I wish she could have taken Lucille's picture.

Four

♣ ♣ ♣

Sara Kate has made Cream of Wheat for breakfast every day this week. She loaded us up with every flavor they made. I still like cinnamon apple the best.

On the back of the package there is a doodle. An easy way to draw an elephant is shown. You can do it even if you can't draw a straight line.

At the peach stand I follow the directions and draw a perfect elephant. I hide it behind my back when Everleen wants to see what I've done. If she Sees it I'll be drawing elephants for the rest of my life. It will make her think I'm gifted and talented. I sure hate that they put that in people's minds about little kids. They never let you play anymore.

I like the man's picture on the Cream of Wheat box. He looks just like my grandpa. I guess my grandpa is still roaming around looking for that mansion in the sky they said he was going to go to. If he finds it I'm sure he'll get a room for me. That is, if there is any truth to that. I'm not so sure about that thing.

Everleen tells Daniel to put down the terrapin he's turning over and over in his hand. "If he bites you, he won't turn you loose until it thunders," she says, looking up at the cloudless sky. Daniel throws the terrapin down.

My uncle tells me to stack empty peach baskets. I hate to, I always hurt my hand. But I do it. Jim Ed is so worried about this peach crop I don't want to put another frown on his face. It wouldn't have any place to go, anyhow. His face is all filled up.

A late spring freeze caused the peaches to have split-seeds. That means that once the seed of a peach freezes, the peach will split wide open as soon as it starts to get ripe. When customers complain about the way the peaches look, Aunt Everleen will tell them right quick, "That's the Lord's work."

It's a real slow day at the stand. Everleen jumps to her feet when a brand new pickup truck pulls up. "I see you have Elberta peaches on your sign," the man says.

"Yes, we do," Everleen brags. "It's the finest canning peach there is. Del Monte cans Elbertas. Says so right on the can."

"Oh, I was just wanting some to eat," the customer says.

"It's the finest eating peach there is," Everleen put in quickly. She rubs one on her big fluffy shirt, and takes a big bite. "This is truly the best peach I ever tasted."

She stuffs the money he gives her into her pocket. He is a physicist down at the nuclear plant. I put his peck of peaches in his truck.

Everleen is reading the newspaper. "Just listen to this," she says. "This little girl is not even nine years old, and she's . . ." She didn't have to finish telling me. I know it's a story about some little girl doing something great. My aunt has never forgotten that Samantha Smith of Maine was invited to Russia because of a letter she wrote.

Everleen thinks if I write Mrs. Reagan I might get invited to the White House. We've been too busy with my spelling, though.

I go and get the dictionary out of the truck before she tells me to. She makes me spell five pages a day, winter or summer. "I think I'm going to have you do your C's again, Clover. You seem to have had a hard time with them." I believe I had a hard time spelling them because she had a hard time saying them. "If a C you should espy," I chant, "place the E before the I."

I watch Everleen's lips move as she whispers C-A-U-C-A-S-I-A-N. She can't whisper worth a hoot. All I have to do to spell it right is to spell after her. Finally she says, "Kak-kah-sin." "C-A-U-C-A-S-I-A-N," I spell. "My mother is a member of the Caucasian race."

She jumps up to give me a big hug, and knocks over a bushel of peaches. Peaches fly everywhere. There is a peach jigsaw puzzle on the ground. Everleen cuts me a really big piece of pineapple-coconut cake. She dances her way through the spilled peaches. "Washington, D.C., make room for Clover Lee Hill, 'cause here she comes."

To this day, I wonder if that sentence was right. I wish I could ask Gaten. Everleen doesn't know too much about stuff like that.

I open a can of Pepsi. "You'd better eat with your daddy's wife tonight, Clover," Everleen frowns. "I'm sick and tired of all the junk food your uncle piles in at this stand. If you drink another Pepsi you gonna turn into one. It's not good for you. I believe in a balanced nutritious diet."

Aunt Ruby Helen said Everleen didn't know beans about a balanced meal. Not a woman who cooked macaroni and cheese, corn pudding, fried okra, potato salad, turnip greens, candied yams, and fried chicken for an ordinary Sunday dinner.

I know what the real problem is. It's money. Jim Ed will go to a machine and pay sixty cents apiece for Pepsi. Everleen only buys them from the grocery store when they go on sale.

We've been having a lot of customers come to the stand this year. Everleen says they think they might get a glimpse of that beautiful white woman Gaten married. Jim Ed says it's because the peaches are fifty cents cheaper at our stand.

Before I leave for home Aunt Everleen combs my hair and makes me hide behind some bushes and change into clean clothes. She always keeps me a set of clean stuff, just in case I get dirty.

Everleen starts stacking peck baskets and telling me all the things I should or shouldn't say to Sara Kate. "Now, remember, Clover," she warns, "we never repeat the things we talk about here at the peach shed. This is family talk." Then she turns right around and says, "Now, remember Sara Kate is family, so be nice and tell her her cooking tastes real, real good. You know how white women are. They want you to brag on 'em all the time. To tell them you love 'em. They don't care whether it's the truth or not. So you be nice, baby girl."

Everleen knows good and well I'm not about to tell that woman I love her. I do put some nice peaches in a basket to take her, though.

"Don't you go carrying peaches to her, Clover," Daniel fusses. "Sara Kate don't hit a lick at a black snake all day long. If she wants some peaches she can bring her uppity self up here and get her own peaches. It wouldn't hurt her one bit to help Mama sometimes."

I put the peaches back. I got sense enough to know they are not Daniel's words, they're his mama's. The only thing on his mind and tongue is a dirt bike.

Here of late everybody is getting on my nerves so bad. Clover, do this. Clover, don't do that. Say this to Sara Kate, don't say that. It's no wonder my leg hurts all the time. I guess it knows my heart sure can't hold all the hurt in it. So I guess it's trying to help it out. Everleen says I've lost my hearing, completely lost it.

I might lose what little eyesight I got left

in one eye for real, though. I got some peach spray in it this morning. I washed it out right good, but it still kind of burns. The warning below the poison skeleton on the bag said it could cause blindness if it got into the eyes. I would have hurried up and told Gaten if he'd been here. I know if I tell Sara Kate she'll rush me to the doctor to have it checked out. So would Everleen and Jim Ed. I've made up my mind. I'll tell one of them about it after awhile.

Sara Kate must have known we were talking about her. No sooner than I'd put the peaches back, she wheeled up and threw on her brakes. A cloud of dust blew every-where. Everleen puffed her lips out and pushed them into a wide upsweep over her nostrils. Her mouth looked like a gorilla's mouth.

"Hi, Everleen. Hi, Clover," Sara Kate says.

I say, "Hey."

Everleen pulls her lips down. "Hey, Sara Kate."

A nasty old yellow jacket is sucking away on a piece of candy I laid down. I know better but I still start to smash him.

"Don't kill that yellow jacket," Aunt Everleen fusses. "You know if you kill one of them their whole family will swarm in and try to sting you to death. We may not be as allergic to them as your uncle Jim Ed, but we sure don't need to invite them just because he's not here."

The truth is I did know if you kill one yellow jacket more will come. But I didn't really know why until I read in the newspaper recently that when you squash a yellow jacket they release some kind of chemical, pheromone or something, that signals a defense alarm that alerts other yellow jackets and they swarm in and sting anyone that's around.

Everleen is some kind of mad. All you have to do to tell when she is mad is look at her mouth. She is right pretty when she's not mad. She pulls a towel off her shoulder and starts dusting off peaches right fast. Sara Kate knows she's brushing her off. She turns to me. "I made your favorite supper, Clover, so don't fill up on peaches again."

Poor Sara Kate. She doesn't know it, but it's Everleen's good cooking I'm always filled up with, not peaches.

Sara Kate is trying to be friendly. "The peaches are so-oo pretty."

"Most of 'em is split wide open. And

71

there's no size to 'em. It's a poor crop," Everleen snaps.

"They are kind of small," Sara Kate agrees. "May I take a few of them?"

"You asking me for peaches? Part of this orchard belonged to Gaten Hill. In case you've forgotten, you did marry him."

Sara Kate turned redder than a Dixie-red peach. You can tell when she's mad, too. I guess everybody's got some kind of way of letting you know they're mad without saying so. She starts toward our pickup truck. "Be sure you're home in time for supper, Clover."

"I'll ride back with you," I say. I need to tell her about my eye. Then without so much as a word, she turns back, grabs a peck basket, and marches toward the orchard. She is walking fast, her head high. She is pounding her feet on the hard baked ground harder than necessary.

Everleen rolls her eyes and grunts, "If that woman don't act like she owns this place, I'm not setting here."

When Sara Kate storms back, she just hops into the truck and speeds away. She forgot all about me. Everleen hugs me. A quick but soft hug. "Miss High-and-mighty wouldn't even let you ride home in your daddy's truck." She draws a deep breath and adds softly, "That is, it was his truck." Her eyes fill with tears.

Jim Ed drives up in his pickup. "Don't block what little air is stirring," Everleen fusses. "Park over yonder. The dust just settled down after your high-and-mighty sister-in-law drove from here like a bat out of hell. And here you come raising up another dust storm."

Everleen is having another one of her fussing spells. But her husband won't fuss back. He's scared she may get one of her bad headaches, or get mad and quit on him.

A funeral procession led by a police car with its flashing light passes along the highway. Jim Ed puts his straw hat over his heart and bows his head. Everleen starts to cry all over again. She crosses herself and mumbles something. She doesn't know why she's doing it. It's something she saw on TV and copied it.

"I can't see why you crying, Mama," says Daniel. "The cars got North Carolina tags and all the people are white, you don't even know them people, Mama."

Everleen is really crying hard. "You don't have to know people to feel sorry for them."

In my heart I know she is crying for my daddy, because his brother, Jim Ed, is crying also. I'm going to cry, too.

Sara Kate had the table set real pretty. She put peach leaves around the peaches she picked. It made the peaches look like they were still on the tree.

There was a postcard from my aunt Ruby Helen beside my plate. At the end it read—"P.S. Wish you were here." If I had gone to live with her, I would have been in Bermuda instead of eating Sara Kate's soupy grits and chicken. I sure hate that I told her I had a taste for some grits.

Sara Kate spooned the watery stuff on my plate, and some chicken swimming in tomatoes and green peppers. I drank my ice tea first. Her eyes were all over my face. Darting like the eyes of a trapped rabbit from my eyes to my mouth. The grits slid through my fork like water soup. If she cooks me grits again I will die, just plain die. "Sara Kate," I blurted out, "you sure can't cook grits." Sara Kate was hurt. I could see the red hurt under her skin. She's got the thinnest skin I've ever seen. Her eyes misted over, but she held the tears back.

I remember all the stuff Everleen said

about her. Like white women being so easy to hurt and all. "You have to remember," Everleen had said, "the most of them have been sheltered and petted all their lives. The least little thing just tears them up." I take a bite of the chicken. It's got the strangest taste. But I eat it anyway. "This chicken is some kind of good, Sara Kate, I said.

Sara Kate offers to put more chicken on my plate when I finish. I shake my head, no. "Clover," she says sharply, "you know how your father felt about shaking your head for an answer. Now, would you like more chicken?"

"Uh, uh," I mutter. There was no way I could have gotten a no answer out of my mouth. It was crammed too full of grits and that tomato chicken. That was the first time Sara Kate ever laid something my daddy said on me.

Sara Kate's back had been turned to me when I'd walked into the kitchen. The radio was playing "Song Sung Blue." Her slim body swayed from side to side. A body moving not to music, but to sadness. There is a big difference, you know.

I'd tiptoed up behind her, and shouted, "boo." She jumped like I had scared the living daylights out of her. She wasn't the least bit mad, or scared for that matter. I could see she had been crying. Her green eyes were all puffed up and red. She has started crying an awful lot here of late. Just up and cries for no reason.

Five

♣ ♣ ♣

There is a lot of sadness sewed up in Sara Kate. A sadness I can't figure out. Like it's hidden on some shelf too tall for me to reach. I'm beginning to think it's not because Gaten's gone. It's because she is stuck with me. Now I'm starting to think, maybe I ought to run away. Then maybe she won't be so sad all the time. I can see she's got her own set of sorrow, a set just like mine.

Sometimes I believe she really loved my daddy. It doesn't make me love her more, though. Still, something in me wants to like her—to have her like me, too.

I guess I kind of wish I could play with her like Daniel plays with his mama. He puts his hands over her eyes and in that strange, new, high-pitched voice of his, cranks out, "Guess who?" Everleen will guess and guess till she has to finally give up. Then in that voice that changes every time he opens his mouth, Daniel will say, "It's me, Danny, your son."

If Sara Kate had done some of all the crying she's doing now at Gaten's funeral, she wouldn't have seemed so curious. There wouldn't have been so much talk about how easy she took her husband's death, either. Everleen says white folks don't cry and carry on like we do when somebody dies. They don't love as hard as we do.

We're just different, I guess. Miss Katie's still mourning over Gaten and she's not even kin. After Gaten was killed, she tried to cook but the pans fell to the floor. So she took to her rocking chair. Sometimes I would go and sit on the floor beside her. To tell you the truth, it was about the only place I could find space to sit. Anyway, she made me cry, too. I'm glad she's getting over Gaten.

People in Round Hill don't know it, but Sara Kate didn't really get over Gaten dying as fast as they think she did. Sara Kate was powerfully sad after my daddy died.

After the funeral she lit a candle and sat alone in the dark. I haven't been able to quite figure out why. People I know in Round Hill don't light candles when folks die. I didn't ask Sara Kate about the candle. I didn't even

78

tell Everleen about it, either. I guess, in a strange sort of way, I don't want anybody thinking like, well, that Sara Kate was strange and everything. Maybe in a sly way I was trying to protect Sara Kate even if I can't stand her sometimes. Somehow, I really believe it was because I'm trying to please my dead daddy.

I'll probably find out about this candle business when I'm watching TV. I don't care what people say, you can so learn a lot of stuff from TV.

Daniel said if his grandma had watched enough TV, she would have known that the movie *57 Pick-Up* wasn't about a pickup truck, and would have never gone with him to see it. She liked to have died when they started spitting out all them nasty cuss words. And when the half-naked women started prancing about, she was more ashamed to leave than to stay. So she slid down in her seat, pulled her hat down over closed eyes and prayed and prayed that if the Lord would forgive her that time she'd never set foot in a movie place again.

Sara Kate's got to be bad lonely working in the house all day, all by herself. Sometimes she writes little notes on fancy flowered paper. I never see her mail them. I think she likes the pretty stamp too much to use.

She hurries up and mails the letters to the places that send the pictures of all them little sad-eyed dogs and cats. On the outside of the envelopes they beg, "Will You Please Help Save Them?" I do believe she sends money every time the little pictures come in the mail. It didn't take them people long to find Sara Kate in Round Hill.

Everleen says all white women give money to the animals if they have it to spare. She says it's because they feel so guilty over the way their people treated us. They think by being extra kind to animals, it'll get them into heaven. But Everleen says the Bible says "the animals are born to be destroyed." She thinks the Lord would smile down more on Sara Kate if she took some of that money and helped out the poor children right in Round Hill. Everleen knows her Bible.

I guess if I had extra money I'd feed kids before I'd feed the animals.

Sometimes Sara Kate plays the piano in a room empty now except for one new chair. It's covered in cloth that feels slick. Sara Kate bought it. She calls the cloth chintz. Everything else is pretty much like it was when Grandpa died. He made Gaten promise never to sell the mirrored umbrella and hat stand in the front hall.

I like it when Sara Kate plays. The house seems to come alive. Gaten used to play tapes of the same kind of music. Miss Kenyon used to play classical music also. Maybe that's why Gaten was in love with her too.

That kind of music is great to listen to. But it isn't hitting up on nothing for dance music.

I guess Gaten would have been happy with Sara Kate in this house. I know one thing, if Gaten could see her feeding dogs—much less stray dogs—out of the bowls we eat out of, he would just up and die again.

Sara Kate may think she is so clean, but this letting dogs eat out of dishes will never set with me. Me and Gaten didn't eat after no dogs. I bet if Jim Ed and Everleen knew about all this, they'd never eat a bite in this house.

I don't think Gaten would have liked all those little yellow notes stuck all over the refrigerator, either. Gaten couldn't stand a messed-up place.

I guess in her own way Sara Kate's not all that bad. Everleen even bragged about the way she took care of Aunt Maude. She is my great aunt and is some kind of old.

Well, after she had a stroke, she fell in her kitchen. Trying to stir up her a bite to eat, she said. It was some kind of big bite. Stewed chicken and dumplings, green onion tops and onions smothered in fried fatback drippings, green crowder peas with snaps, cornbread and grated sweet potato pudding. She made the pudding because she wanted to try out a new rum flavor she bought from a Rawleigh Product salesman.

Everleen was going to take her in, but Sara Kate offered, since Everleen was working so hard at the peach shed. That was one time Sara Kate came in real good. I couldn't help out too much with Aunt Maude, because she kept mixing me up. After her stroke her mind was affected. She lost her marbles, that's what happened. She forgot Gaten had been killed. Every day she would say, "Gaten come in yet?" Or she'd say, "Come on, Clover, let me comb your hair. Go and change them dirty clothes. Put on a dress. I want your daddy to see he's got a little girl when he gets home from school." Then she'd tell about the time when she was teaching school. They made a fire in the big wood heater and a big snake crawled out through the grate.

Sara Kate makes mugs of coffee or tea in the microwave, does needlepoint and listens. She picks up enough of Aunt Maude's slurred speech to laugh. Sometimes when she talks about Gaten as a young boy, Sara Kate cries.

Poor Aunt Maude's mind has got to be torn up pretty bad. She's been eating Sara Kate's turnips and things cooked flat-out in water, without a speck of grease. Once she zipped her lips and wouldn't eat. And don't you know Sara Kate fixed up her plate all pretty, dotted the greens with red Jell-o cubes and Aunt Maude ate it. You got to be in mighty bad shape in the head to eat greens and Jell-o.

In no time Sara Kate had nursed her back to health. She got well enough for her daughter to come and take her to Greensboro to live.

Maybe if Sara Kate could get ahold of poor old drunk Gideon she might cure him up. They didn't do a thing for him down at that first place he went to. He is walking down the hot dusty road now, swaying from side to side. He said he's learned AA's twelve steps. It seems like he's taking twenty-three steps to make his twelve. If he keeps on he'll do a solo two-step dance.

Gideon's thin body looked like the frame of an undressed scarecrow. Leaning into the wind, his body traveled faster than his feet. Even so, that body had started to look like it housed a living creature. Gideon had spent seven days in a detox center. He'd been sober all those days and it showed. He showed off a white button he got at the AA meeting. His wife was so proud of him, she said it even tickled her bones.

I am probably kin to Gideon, but not as close kin as he makes us out to be. Good old Aunt Everleen tries to tie us up to as much kinfolk as she can. She stretches out the family line just like she stretches out sadness. She needs kinfolk to worry about, to be sad over, and make unhappiness so big she can save some over, so it'll be handy in case she needs it.

If she could see Gideon right now, she'd just pinch off a little sadness and moan, "Poor Gideon, bless his heart." Then she'd hurry up and bake him a little tin pie-pan cake. She calls it a sample cake. She never bakes a cake unless she makes a couple of samples first. She has to try out one, just in case the cake needs something. I've never seen her add anything to the cake batter. I think she just can't wait until the real cake is done. I love her sample cakes.

For a little while Gideon was sober. But then, that was yesterday. Today he is waving a notice from Duke Power Company. They are going to shut off his lights. Today Gideon is as drunk as a blind cooter.

Sara Kate's bedroom door is closed. It's the room she and my daddy would have slept in. I stand outside for a few minutes trying to think up a way to tell her about getting poison in my eye. I clean forgot to tell her at suppertime. I'm only planning to tell her now because, now that I think about it, it's my good eye that got the poison in it.

I doubt if Sara Kate knows I don't see all that good out of one of my eyes as it is. That is, when I don't wear my eyeglasses. I hardly ever wear them. My glasses are hidden in Gaten's bottom desk drawer. I never could stand to wear the things. Like I told Gaten, "One eye will see enough of everything I need to see."

I cannot believe Gaten would have told Sara Kate about my eye. I imagine, like me, he would have thought it was something she didn't necessarily need to know.

85

When I finally knock on Sara Kate's door, there is no answer. I guess I did knock kind of soft. But I don't go around knocking on people's doors that much.

Gaten closed his bedroom door if he was getting dressed or something. I'm almost sure he didn't close it when he was ready to go to sleep. I kind of think he left it open so he could hear me if I was having a bad dream or something. He also had to know that ever since Grandpa died, I've been a little scared at night.

I knock again and again. In my heart I know I am knocking too softly and I know why. I really don't want her to hear me. As sure as shooting, if I tell her about my eye, she'll rush me off to the hospital. Besides, my eye had stopped burning anyway. Even so, I still splashed cold water into it until I couldn't stand it anymore.

The first thing Everleen wants to know the next day is how Sara Kate's dinner turned out. I say it was awful, that the grits were plain nasty. "That's not nice to say, Clover," she fussed. I can tell she's glad I didn't say it was all that good. I can tell you, she wants to be tops in the cooking department.

"You and Daniel, get outta the sun before

you have a heat stroke, Clover," she warned us. "Anytime you have them old cicadas singing so strong this early in the day, you know it's gonna be a scorcher. They said on the evening news last night this is the hottest, driest summer we ever had in South Carolina . . .

"You know it's got to be bad here, when we make the big-time news . . . thank the Lord all them Northerners are trucking down hay, 'cause if it gets any worse . . ."

I move into the shade. Daniel and his daddy go to buy fuel oil. They're tired of listening to Everleen.

I think about Sara Kate. All alone in our quiet house. Thinking her quiet thoughts, writing quiet words. Daniel wants me to sneak out some of that writing. He thinks it might be stuff about us.

Once or twice I started into Sara Kate's room to slip the papers she'd written out. Each time something inside me stopped me. Maybe it was the hand of an angel. My grandpa used to pray for the angels to watch over me. I believe in angels.

I've known for a long time to never, ever mess with Sara Kate's drawings. Once I picked up some of the pretty little sketches on drawing paper, and forgot and left them out on the back door steps.

We looked everywhere for the sketches. We even took everything out of her big zippered artist portfolio. It's more like a briefcase for a giant. I just had a notion the sketches may have been there, but we never did find them. The white Federal Express truck came and left without them.

Well, Sara Kate was really, really angry with me that time. And she didn't mind letting me know it, either. "Clover," she fussed, "those sketches were to be sent to a company who wants me to design a line of fancy wrapping paper. I spoke with a man from the company and promised him he'd have the sketches tomorrow. There is good money in that, Clover, and right now we can use it."

Her mad spell didn't last too long. But, oh boy, let me tell you something, when a white woman gets mad, she gets mad.

Sara Kate finally smiled and sucked in her breath when I said, "Well, Sara Kate, maybe the next day won't be too late. If you had all them pretty flowers and things in your head in the first place you ought to be able to find them again. At least we can find your head. It's not lost, that's for sure."

I still can't see how Sara Kate can stand so much sitting down all the time. If she isn't drawing or painting, she's writing. No wonder her hips are so flat.

Anyway, I've left the papers alone for good. If Sara Kate is writing something bad about us, I don't want to find out.

A little girl about my age is screaming at her mama to hurry up and buy the peaches so they can go to McDonalds. She has blue, blue eyes and hair I guess they call blonde. It sure looks white to me, though.

"Please wait, darling," says her mama sweetly, "we'll go as soon as I buy the peaches."

"I don't like peaches," the little girl screams. "I hate peaches."

I put a peck of peaches on the back seat of their car, one of them new Toyota jobs. The white-haired girl sticks her tongue out at me. I stick mine out right back at her. She makes a face as they drive away. All I can say is, if she does that to me at school, she'll get her lights punched out. She'll probably go to one of those private church schools they started setting up when the public schools started getting so many black principals.

Gideon's sister and her husband thought after they got high-paying jobs at Duke Power Company they would send their kids to one of those schools. But Everleen said the good old Baptists had no room for good old black Baptists. And to this day, there is not a single black there.

About a half mile up the road, the signal light on an old Buick blinks for a left turn. A line of cars and eighteen-wheeled trucks brake and screech behind the Buick, slowly snaking its way to the turnoff.

"Lord? Lord," Everleen groans, "Mary Martha is gonna get herself run clean over, crawling along that busy highway. A cooter could travel faster than that."

Mary Martha has to put both feet on the ground and hold onto the door frame in order to pull her fat body out of the car. She has the body of a woman, but her face is a girl's face.

"I don't know why I'm buying peaches," she complained. "I'm so tired of working in these poor white folks' kitchens, I ain't got the strength to make a pie."

"Huh," Everleen grunts, "you and Miss Katie's the only ones still doing it that I know of."

"I know, I know. But, Everleen, what else

can I do? I'm too worn out to go into one of the mills to work. James Roy's got a right good job, but we got not one, but four chaps to get ready for school. To tell you the truth, I need another little job."

Everleen tilts her head upwards and laughs about something that's making her tickled before she says it. She's really pretty when she laughs. She wears her long black hair pulled back off her dark-skinned face, and has the prettiest eyes you ever saw. "The blacker the berry, the sweeter the juice," she says about her dark skin color.

Everleen is still laughing. "I hear tell Miss Sara Kate Hill is looking for somebody to clean her house. Like she's some kind of rich white woman."

Mary Martha shakes her head. "Girl, I may be hard up, but I'd eat water and bread before I set foot in that woman's house to clean. To this day I ain't got over Gaten marrying her instead of Miss Kenyon. Seems like every time one of our fine girls have the chance for a good catch, some cracker comes along and messes it up. I'll bet the new white principal who took Gaten's place won't marry one of our black teachers."

"He won't marry a white one, either," Everleen says. They both laugh.

They wave at a passing car and moan, "Oh Lordy, Lord." It's Rooster Jones, breezing by in his brand new Pontiac.

"I'm surprised he even waved with his fine self," Mary Martha says. "Talk in town is, he's started taking up with them trashy white gals with their long dirty hair, thin lips, and slim hips. They hang around the mill every night. He'll lose the shirt off his back now."

"Girl, you are telling the Lord's truth," says Everleen, shaking her head. "If our menfolk make a plug nickel, they get the hots for them. And Lordy me, if they can shoot a basketball, those girls trail behind them like a hound dog running a coon. And when they catch them, they cling to them tighter than a green cocklebur."

"Either that, or they wise up, get their teeth fixed, and get all gussied up, then marry some old man of their own race, in his eighties with more money than they can spend. They can then live so grand, they can make their born rich sisters look pitiful, pitiful."

Everleen may be kind to Sara Kate's face, but she sure can't stand her behind her back.

They start talking about my daddy again. They must have forgotten that I was sitting right there all the time. They can't know how much it hurts me to have them talk like that about my own daddy. I thought that all the talk about Sara Kate and Gaten would all be over by now. Before Gaten died, I had to listen to all the talk he and his brother did.

People in Round Hill may not know it, but my daddy didn't just up and marry the woman with no thought. It wasn't even an easy thing for him to do. It gnawed at his gut. And my actions sure didn't help, either. I would be so different now if I had the chance. It's too late now. My daddy is dead.

I happen to know my daddy thought long and hard before he married Sara Kate. Maybe if all these women knew what the man went through, they would stop talking so bad about him.

I am only ten years old, but certainly old enough to know that my daddy had to make a choice. There is nothing else you can do, when you have people pulling at you from every side. One thing is for sure, you can't go with everybody at the same time. So Gaten had to make a choice.

I still think of the day he brought his lady to meet me. Gaten was nervous. More so than I had ever seen him. I may not know a lot of things, but I do know a lot about my daddy's ways.

The eyes of the woman by his side clocked his every move. She was waiting for him to tell me something. Gaten tried to, but he seemed as if he could not speak. His tongue seemed to press against his teeth. He stood mute before us. I suppose he wasn't prepared for the way I treated his lady. I could tell, he really wanted me to take to her. He should have known you just can't cram that kind of thing inside a person's head and mind and make them like someone no matter what.

I cannot understand why Gaten always seemed to think I needed extra help in being raised, anyway. All my life, as far back as I can remember, I've just had one person at a time. First it was my grandpa before he died. And then I had Gaten.

When I was little I was alone with my grandpa most of the time. My uncle and aunt were in and out of the house every single day, but they didn't live with us. My daddy came home almost every weekend.

After I started going to school my daddy wanted to take me away to live with him. He was teaching school somewhere around Charleston, South Carolina. He claimed Grandpa had been too easy with me. Allowed me to pick up wrong habits. Gaten hated for me to spit and use coarse words.

Grandpa didn't teach me that kind of stuff. I learned it from my cousin Daniel. The one thing Gaten didn't really like was, I missed a lot of days at school. It was true that Grandpa did not make me go to school all that much. He said it didn't matter if I missed a few days here and there. I had the rest of my life to go to school.

To this day I believe it was my aunt Everleen who put it into Gaten's head to come and take me way down there to live with him.

I started crying when Gaten called to say he was coming for me. School or no school, I couldn't see how my daddy could begin to think of splitting up me and my grandpa. I couldn't have gone and lived away from Aunt Everleen, anyway. Who in the world would have fixed my hair? I've always been tender-headed. I've never liked people fooling with my hair.

I kind of believe my grandpa was crying also. He sucked-up real hard through his nose and wiped it with the back of his hand. I can never tell by his eyes if he is crying. He is getting kind of old and his eyes look watery all the time, anyway.

At first, Grandpa had said to my daddy, "But son, she's all I got. I just don't think I am prepared to lose her right now." In the end, though, all he said was, "I will have my baby girl ready and waiting when you come for her."

Breakfast was on the table when my daddy walked into the house. We had grits, ham and eggs, and red-eye gravy. Grandpa had spread butter and Aunt Everleen's home-made blackberry jelly on hot biscuits as soon as he took them out of the oven.

All the time we were eating breakfast, I didn't raise my head to look at my daddy. Every now and then, I did cut my eyes up to glance at him. Each time he was looking dead at me. My aunt had really fixed me up. My hair was pulled into a pony tail with a big purple bow. It matched my new purple flowered dress, with puffed sleeves and a little white pique bib in front.

I dug little ditches in my plate of hot grits and watched yellow melted butter run through like little streams of water.

When Grandpa passed my daddy the hot biscuits for the umpteenth time, he tipped the Ball mason jar with the wildflowers I'd picked, and water spilled all over the red-checkered tablecloth.

Grandpa blotted up the water with a dish towel. "You might know Clover picked these weeds, I mean flowers. The child is a spitting image of her departed mama. Even when there was snow on the ground, her mama found red berries or something to pick and put on this table. This house hasn't been the same without her."

He could never stand to talk very much about my mama. He said he loved her like she was his own daughter. I guess he now felt he was about to lose me, too. He was sad and started to cry. Real tears streamed down into the lines and wrinkles of his brown leathery face.

I sure never remembered seeing all those wrinkles in his face before. My daddy said, "Old age made them." I guess day by day old age was using its hand to carefully draw them on. "Oh Lord, oh Lord," he cried out, "help me, because I am weak. Send me your mercy to lean on."

Like lickety-split, I was by my grandpa's side. I put my arms around his neck. "Don't worry, Grandpa," I said. "You will always have me to lean on, for as long as I live."

I hadn't said more than two words to my daddy up to then. But now I was ready to lay some kind of fussing on him. "I'm mad now," I fussed. "Really mad. You know for yourself that poor old Grandpa can't bit more take care of himself than a newborn baby. You ought to be ashamed of yourself, Gaten, to even think of taking the only help he's got in this world away." I just had to call my daddy Gaten, because for some reason the word daddy would not come out of my mouth.

I didn't know what my daddy was thinking. All I did know was, he looked at my grandpa—his own daddy—and he had to see what I saw. An old, feeble man. His eyes were even old. There was hardly any color left in them. It's strange that I'd never paid any attention to his teeth before. They looked as though they had been sawed off. Years and years of chewing had sawed them down, the same way old age had brought his voice down. A voice not half as strong as it used to be.

My daddy must have seen what I saw, because tears welled up in his eyes. Without a word, he walked into the hall, picked up my two packed suitcases, and the burlap sack that Grandpa packed for me. Only the Lord in the heavens knows what was in that sack. Anyhow, they stood waiting and ready near the front door. My daddy carried them back upstairs.

A year later, my daddy was home for good. A principal's job at the Round Hill Elementary School opened up, and my daddy got the job. The only problem for me was, it was my school. I guess that's what turned me around for good from calling my father "Daddy." I sure didn't feel right calling him Mr. Hill. So I called him Gaten. Besides, that's what everybody else in our family called him.

Things sure can happen fast in a person's life. Grandpa was dead and buried. And there was Gaten, all hurt and sad on account of a complete stranger, a woman named Sara Kate.

Uncle Jim Ed and Gaten were sitting on the front porch, talking about all they ever seem to talk about, the peach crop.

"Speak of the devil . . ." Jim Ed laughs when Chase Porter drives up. They all laugh.

"We were just talking about you, Chase, and wondering if you might have a spare spray machine belt. I had to stop short rounding a curve at full speed when I was spraying and the belt snapped." Gaten looked at his brother. "Jim Ed had left our fuel can right in the middle of a row."

Chase grinned. "I wouldn't have wanted to hear about what you said. I do have an extra belt, and come to think of it, I'm sending someone to Spartanburg tomorrow to get some parts. You can send for whatever you need if you want to."

"Well, that was perfect timing," Gaten said when Chase left.

"Speaking of timing," Uncle Jim Ed said, "I have asked you three times if we are going to spray peaches in the morning. I have yet to get a straight answer from you."

"Yep, we've got to spray all right," Gaten agreed. "I'll fix up the spray machine with water, and have it ready."

Uncle Jim Ed got up to leave. "I'll take care of the spray machine, big boy. It seems like you've got a lot on your mind today."

Gaten looked at the house. "The old home place is beginning to run down, Jim Ed. Needs painting. It's turning gray. Even the flowers seem to be struggling to hold onto the little life left in them."

Jim Ed laughed. "At least it's only the trimming that needs to be done. The old brick still looks pretty good. Remember the imitation brick siding that used to be on it?

I was so glad when Papa agreed to take it off and put up real bricks." He glanced at the flowers. "You would be struggling to hold onto life, too, if you were as old as some of these flowers. Mama said she set out those crape myrtle and rose bushes right after she was married. I guess the hollyhocks and verbenas have kept reseeding over the years. You and Miss Katie are the only ones who have them." His face showed a trace of re-membered sadness. He walked to a small bush. His hand gently touched the leaves. That same bush would later bloom forth with soft pink blossoms, clustered into little balls of petals that scatter and fall like silent snowflakes.

He looked at Gaten. "We sure well re-member who set this one out." Gaten looked at me. My mother set the bush out, just before she died. She had planted lots of things, but it was the only one that lived. She called it a marble bush.

Jim Ed made a play in the hopscotch game I'd drawn in a sandy spot at the edge of our yard. "TV hasn't changed the playing pat-tern of our little Clover too much," he said. "She still plays some of the same things we did when we were growing up." He shook his head sadly. "I can't pry that kid of mine away from the tube."

Gaten smiled. "Clover may be a child of the eighties, but the same person of the twenties that raised us, raised her also."

"I've got to get a move on," Jim Ed said, stopping to take one last look at the old brick house with shutters and dormer windows. "The house is still in great shape. I only wish mine was half as fine." He frowned and looked directly at Gaten. "I know it's something else that's really bothering you, younger brother. I can tell, you are hurting, man."

When Jim Ed called Gaten "younger brother," Gaten knew he meant for him to listen because he was older. They said as soon as Gaten could talk, he told everyone not to call him baby brother.

It didn't seem to bother Gaten one bit that I was listening to every word. He must have wanted me to hear.

"I've never been able to handle hurt, Jim Ed. Especially when it involves people I love so much," he said.

I climbed out on a limb on our old chinaberry tree. "Look, Jim Ed," I laughed, swinging from my legs, "no hands, no hands."

"Get down out of that tree this minute, Clover," Gaten ordered. There was a sharpness in his voice that even shocked Jim Ed.

"Let her play," he said, "she is still only a little girl."

"That's exactly the point," Gaten snapped. "It's high time she started acting like she is a little girl. Clover has gotten out of hand here of late. I am not proud of the kind of person she is becoming."

Jim Ed studied my daddy for a long time. "It' that woman, all right," he finally said. "She has changed everything about you. You have changed the way you feel about your very own child. Up until you met her, Clover could do no wrong in your eyes. If you are not careful, that woman will wind up destroying you." My uncle was stepping on his brother's toes all right. Gaten's face showed it.

"I don't care, younger brother, if it makes you mad or not. To tell you the truth, I don't give a . . ." he glanced at me and stopped short. He and Gaten both know how to curse as good as a drunk sailor. Gaten doesn't curse in my presence, and he sure won't stand for someone else doing it.

"I am just going to come out with it, Gaten," Jim Ed went on. "That woman is about to drive you storm crazy. What you don't know is, unlike our womenfolk, those women don't part easily with something they want. You happen to be a pretty good catch. And, in spite of all the odds, that woman wants you."

Through closed jaws, Gaten is gritting his teeth. His jaws are working like a chainsaw cutting through maple wood. "Do you care to tell me how you happened to become so experienced in this kind of situation, Jim Ed? Have you gone through a similar thing before?" His voice was hard and cruel. He did not try to hide it, either.

"You don't have to cut me up," Jim Ed said quietly. "If you want to get tied up with someone like that woman, it's your business. All I can say is, it's a heavy, heavy load to dump on our little Clover. She has had so much sadness in her short lifetime. Now that she is barely, just barely, getting over her grandfather's death, she sure does not need some stranger in her life to have to get used to."

"Whew," I thought to myself. Jim Ed better back off. He is making Gaten some kind of mad. If he keeps on, Gaten is going to blow his stack. I also think, perhaps the reason it's so hard for me to get over stuff is because people keep telling me that I can't, or am not, getting over it.

Jim Ed did not back off. "Nowadays, women like her are starting to set their hooks to catch any black guy that's worth a little something. Especially now that so many are starting to make their way up in the world. As far as they are concerned, all they ever need to see is the dollar sign. I'm not saying that you have anything, but there is no denying that you have always been an achiever. A 'first.' The youngest winner ever, of a statewide oratorical contest. Also the 'first' black to win that honor. The 'first' black principal at a Round Hill school. I have yet to learn if 'what-you-may-call-her' even has a job."

Gaten is still as mad as a striking rattlesnake. He has always known how to keep it in. I am not quite sure how he does it. It might be in the way he keeps his voice down.

He eyes his brother. "Sara Kate Colson is a college graduate. Yes, she does work. She is a textile designer."

I can see Jim Ed sure didn't know what kind of work that was. I didn't, either, and Gaten sure was not about to tell us. I'm not sure, but I think Jim Ed was not too pleased to hear that, on account of his wife Everleen not having too much schooling.

"If you are thinking Sara Kate is some fly-by-night I just happened to bump into, you are dead wrong, Jim Ed."

Gaten and my uncle seemed to be heading for yet another round in their fight.

"How could I have known," Gaten said, "that posting one little note, 'Math Tutor—Affordable Rates' would have led to this. Sara Kate Colson was the first and only one who called. I must admit I was kind of taken with her. Unlike most of us at Clemson University, she didn't really seem to belong there. It was not all that unusual, though, that after a term at Parsons School of Design she would choose Clemson. She was so into textiles and design, and Clemson happened to offer one of the foremost textile programs in the country."

Jim Ed looked at Gaten. He seemed to know that Gaten wanted to talk, so he let him go on.

Gaten pulled his face into a serious frown. "I guess I was drawn to Sara Kate when in time I realized she actually didn't need help with math. I hate to admit it, but she was just as good as I was in math, if not better.

Now, to beat me at that time was saying something.

"I decided she only sought help in order to free her mind to cope with an unpleasant turn of events. Her very reason for coming to Clemson turned sour. The guy she cared enough about to follow there ended up getting engaged to someone else. To this day I cannot understand how anyone could have given her up. She is so special."

A wide grin crossed Jim Ed's face. "So you decided to move in?"

My daddy shook his head. "I didn't even try it. I think we both were aware that something beyond just friendship could have developed between us, but we consciously avoided the possibility. At least I did. The time was not ripe for us. Not in South Carolina at least. So, after college, we went our separate ways."

Gaten turned his gaze towards the flower bush my mother had planted. He's thinking about my mama, I thought to myself. I was right. He was. "Besides," he added softly, "I was hopelessly in love with Berenda."

Gaten loved my mother all right. But now she was gone, and a new woman was taking over his life. He couldn't stop talking about her.

"Maybe she was drawn to me," he went on to say, "because I listened to her pour out her heart, and did her homework. Can you believe that sometimes she corrected me, her tutor?"

Gaten looked directly at Jim Ed. "You know something, she paid me anyway."

Jim Ed grunted, "And of course you took it."

Gaten's voice was sad, really sad. "I had to, Jim Ed. You know how badly I needed the money. I was living on a shoestring."

Jim Ed propped his leg upon the tongue of the spray machine, and leaned an elbow on his knee. "How well I remember," he said, looking across the land. "That's why Boot Ellis's house sits on land that used to belong to us. Papa sold him that land to help pay your tuition. Those were pretty hard times back then."

Gaten agreed. "In spite of it all, Papa still seemed to have a Midas touch. When everyone else was losing their crops and farms, he held onto his. The very fact that he could not afford to buy fertilizer one year was the reason we turned to organic farming. When that Clemson county agent checked my 4-H farming project, he couldn't believe what he saw. And Papa couldn't believe it when I got that scholarship, either. He wanted me to learn how to farm in the summer, and hold a job in the winter. Teaching school was the answer."

Jim Ed laughed. "Papa always did say there was nothing finer for farming than an old-fashioned horse-and-cow-manure mixture."

It seemed that no sooner had the two of them started getting along so good, than they quickly changed courses and started arguing again. I believe my uncle hated to see my daddy get tied up with the woman worse than I did.

It all ended up with them fussing over money. Uncle Jim Ed claimed that Gaten's education had not only cost him money, but his own education as well. I hated to hear them fuss over money.

Miss Katie said money was a bad thing, and according to the good book, it was the root of all evil. There had to be a lot of truth to that because money sure caused Gaten and Jim Ed to turn mighty evil.

Gaten seemed all tired out. His mind is all messed up, I can tell. Gaten sighed. "We all know what the real problem about Sara Kate is. Even in the eighties, we are still reluctant to address it. You know something, that is a sad, sad thing."

Jim Ed kicked the dusty ground. "I guess the thing that bothers me most is what people around here will say." He looked directly at Gaten. "And you know what they will say. We will never know how Berenda would have felt about this."

It hurt Gaten when he mentioned Berenda. It hurt me too. She was my mother. "Berenda is dead, Jim Ed," Gaten finally said in a quiet voice. A voice now drained of all its anger.

Jim Ed still had to stir the pot again. To have the last word. "If you ever allow your mind to free your thoughts to think over what you are about to get into, you will find the answer, and make the right choice, Gaten."

I never thought I would see the day Jim Ed and Gaten would turn against each other. Yet it was happening. Miss Katie said one of the signs of the end of the world would be when brother would turn against brother. Right before my very eyes, a wall had gone up between them. The end must be near. If I had a brother, or a sister for that matter, I would stick with them, through thick and thin, no matter what.

It ended up bad between them. They parted mad, two brothers set apart by anger. Separated, all because of a woman named Sara Kate.

"That old rain crow keeps on hollering," I said to Gaten after Uncle Jim Ed left. "I think I am going to look for him. Grandpa said this time of day is a good time to look for one, if you ever hope to spot one."

An old stray dog had wandered into our yard. He followed me as I started to walk away. Down the path a piece of way I stopped but didn't turn around to look back at Gaten. "Could be a big, big snake down there for all I know," I called back.

"Listen, Gaten," I continued, "there goes the rain crow again. It's a good thing Aunt Everleen took her wash off the line. We might get a gully-washer, right?" When Gaten wouldn't open his mouth, I couldn't help myself. I had to fuss at him. "If you would swallow some of that anger all swelled up inside your mad self, Gaten, you would be able to talk to somebody when they talk to you."

I started to walk away again. Every now and then I'd turn my head a little to see if, by chance, he'd decided to come with me. He didn't.

Near the edge of the woods, when I took a path through a shallow gully, overgrown with creeping kudzu vines, I heard Gaten call out, "Hey, little stranger, wait up."

"I'm looking for my little girl," he said when he caught up. He looked at the tears streaming down my face. "She wasn't crying when I saw her last. Perhaps you may have seen my little, smiling daughter?" I broke into a wide grin. I loved my daddy when he was playful. "What does she look like?" I asked.

Gaten frowned and made a serious face. "Well, now, let me see." With his hand he measured height. "She's about this tall," he said. "Her face is a little chocolate chip with big velvet brown eyes. There is a haunting beauty in the way her eyes seem to tease the lips of a perfect little mouth into an ever ready smile. She has a little button nose. Even though she is always too eager to turn it up in disgust, it's still perfect. She is a very beautiful little girl."

"What was she wearing, Mister?" I asked.

"A pair of blue jeans, torn on both knees, and a little blue tee shirt with strawberry popsicle stains all over the front."

I started to giggle. "That's me, Gaten, you've found me."

Gaten looked closely at me. He brushed dirt from my face, then with make-believe surprise said, "Oh, it is you, Clover." He grabbed my hand. His strong hand held it tightly. It was a father's hold. I was safe with him. In the evening twilight we walked hand in hand in search of the very-hard-to-find rain crow.

Everleen is whispering something I cannot hear. Not that I want to. If in the beginning it had been news to her that her husband Jim Ed didn't want his brother to get tied up with Sara Kate, I sure couldn't tell it when I told her what had happened between the brothers. All she said was, "People need to be accepted and judged by the kind of person they are inside, not on the basis of the color of their skin."

In a way, it seemed like she was kind of in favor of Gaten and Sara Kate getting together. But then you can't always guess Everleen. Lots of times she says what she doesn't mind hearing repeated in the streets. That does not mean it is necessarily what's in her heart. At least that's what my daddy always said about her.

Right now I can't stand having to sit here and listen to two people put down my daddy.

It's too soon to tell if talk about Sara Kate will in time hurt me as bad. Even now, there is a little tinge of hurt or sadness when they talk so bad about her.

I get up to leave, but my leg really hurts a lot, so I limp a little and sort of drag it along. "Pick up that leg and walk right, Clover," Everleen calls out after me. "I heard once there was a little girl who dragged her leg like that. Just sliding it along like you are doing. I've asked you time and again if that leg was aching you, and every time you've said, 'No, Aunt Everleen,' then you pick it up and walk.

"Well anyway, don't you know, one day that very child turned into a snake, crawled into the bushes and vanished."

My leg still hurts, but I pick it up and walk on it anyway. I don't care how bad it hurts when I bear down on it. I can't stand having Everleen tell me that turning-into-a-snake story.

If my daddy had had any idea how much sadness his marrying Sara Kate, then up and dying, was putting me through, I don't believe he would have done it. Just living with Sara Kate is strange enough, much less having to listen to everybody talk about your daddy.

I'm not calling my daddy a fool or anything like that. All I'm saying is he up and did a fool thing when he married Sara Kate. It's true what everyone says, "Gaten just turned a fool when he met Sara Kate."

Six

♣ ♣ ♣

An unfinished jigsaw puzzle is spread out on our dining room table. Sara Kate has arranged fresh cut flowers real pretty and placed them throughout the house. Sunlight cuts through half-closed curtains. There is the smell of food cooking, the sound of good music fills the house.

At a glance the house seems to be just a warm, ordinary household. Like the kind you see on television, a house filled with pretty things and a happy family. But after a little while what is real sweeps through, like the smell of Sara Kate's perfume sifts from room to room.

It becomes real that there is something about our house that is not all that happy. It kind of reminds me of a thick morning fog. It's there, you can see it, yet you can't put your finger on it. Like the fog, a strange, uneasy feeling has filled the house, and settled down upon us.

There is just the two of us. A stepmother and child. Two people in a house. Together, yet apart. Aside from the music, the house is too quiet. We move about in separate ways. We are like peaches. Peaches picked from the same tree, but put in separate baskets.

I guess you would call me a scared little girl, all alone with a scared woman. I suppose there is nothing all that strange about a stepmama and a stepchild living alone. In our case, I guess it's just how we happened to end up together.

People get killed every day, get stepmothers all the time. But in this case it all happened on the same day. Only minutes after my daddy married Sara Kate he was killed.

So here we are. Two strangers in a house. I think of all the things I'd like to say to her. Think of all the things I think she'd like to say to me. I do believe if we could bring ourselves to say those things it would close the wide gap between us and draw us closer together. Yet the thoughts stay in my head —stay tied up on my tongue.

Maybe my stepmother has the same fear I have, a fear of not being accepted. In a way it reminds me of a game of Monopoly.

If Sara Kate and I ever forget who we are,

and sometimes we do, then we are at ease with each other and we have a pretty good little time together. Sometimes we even laugh.

Just maybe we could learn something from each other. Especially Sara Kate since she's the one new to the house. At least she will learn that the sound that sometimes goes boom in the night is only a shutter slamming shut. All houses have their own creaky sounds.

Right now there is hardly a sound in the house. It is so very, very dry. The drought has sucked up all the wind. Just like in the poem . . . "No wind, no rain, no motion." It's been so hot, Mr. Barnes' old rooster has stopped crowing. It seems it's even been too hot for the crickets and insects to join the nightly choir and sing.

You just wait until the fall comes. Sara Kate is going to be scared out of her wits for sure when the hoot owl cranks up. It even gives me the chills. My grandpa couldn't stand to hear the hoot owl. He used to turn a boot upside down on the fireplace hearth to quiet it down.

I guess if Sara Kate ever saw that, she'd think she had married into a completely crazy family. She probably thinks it already.

I think the wake they held before Gaten's funeral all but blew her away.

On the other hand, I'm sure there are things I can learn from Sara Kate. Like what she's thinking when she purses her lips, knits her brow together and stares blankly out of the window. I just might learn that in spite of her curious ways, she might want to be my friend—that in some small way, she might even like me.

If I had answered the telephone and hung up when I was supposed to, I would have never been trapped into listening in on Sara Kate's conversation with her mother. I still don't believe I would have eavesdropped if she hadn't laid the phone down. "Hold on a second, Mother," she said. "I must take my muffins out of the oven." Baking muffins happens to be something Sara Kate likes to do. She can make pretty ones, all right. They look like a picture in a magazine. They might would taste as good as they look, and be fit to eat, if she ever learns to put enough sugar in them.

I wanted to hang up when Sara Kate picked the phone up again, but all I needed was to have her think that I was listening on purpose. She may have thought I made it a habit to listen to her phone calls. I had sense enough to know I could not set that phone down without her knowing it. So you see I was truly trapped. I honestly had no choice but to listen.

Sara Kate seemed delighted that her mother had called. "Why don't you come down for a visit, Mother?" she asked after they'd talked for awhile.

"Why, my darling," her mother said in that same rushed, girlish voice Sara Kate has, "I've gotten things all ready for you to spend some time here. You surely have no reason to stay there now."

"There is a child, Mother."

"Oh my God," her mother gasped, "please don't tell me there is a child on the way. Don't give me a heart attack. Say you are not pregnant, Sara Kate."

"Mother, I am not pregnant. Remember, Gaten had a child. A little girl."

There was a deadly silence on the phone. A cold silence without an ounce of feeling in it.

"Come to think of it, dear, I do remember your mentioning it," said her mother.

Sara Kate's voice sounded far, far away. "Gaten's daughter is named Clover. She is a precocious ten-year-old. A darling little girl. But I must admit, it's quite a challenge for me to learn how to care for a ten-year-old."

"I'm afraid I can't help you there, dear. You see, I've never had a ten-year-old step-child. Besides, she is really not your . . ." Her mother's voice broke off. She didn't finish the sentence, there was no need to.

"Well, if you remember, Sara Kate," her mother continued, "from the very beginning, I warned you to take a long hard look at the price you may have to pay for what you called love. Then ask yourself if it was worth it. If love happens to carry problems, then find someone without them. Problems take away love. That was and still is my advice for you."

"Good-bye, Mother," whispered Sara Kate. She then eased the receiver down so gently it hardly made a click. Maybe she was trying to prove to herself how cool she could be.

When she passed me in the hall rushing to her room I could see silent tears creeping down her face. Sara Kate had tears, but she wasn't crying. It seemed like the same air of sadness that filled her lungs when Gaten died was vacuuming her crying into its silent self.

Maybe her mama was right. Maybe Sara

Kate didn't have a reason to stay in Round Hill.

I hope Sara Kate is not sad she got tied up with Gaten and ended up with me. I hate it when she is sad like that. It's really hard on me. Because, you see, a lot of the time, actually, most of the time, I'm sad also. Really sad.

Seven

♣ ♣ ♣

It sure surprised Sara Kate more than it did me when Chase Porter showed up at our house one Sunday afternoon.

I think he started liking her the first time he saw her. And to think Sara Kate wasn't even pretty then, like she is now. Purple and black bruises, fringed with white flesh, were all over her. She looked like a Band-Aid jigsaw puzzle. After all, it was only three days after the car wreck.

I watched Chase peep in his pickup mirror, run a comb through his hair and reach for his hat. He is some fine.

He told Sara Kate that he used to always come to our house when Gaten was alive. "Gaten was my friend," he said. But as far as this friend bit goes, they were not all that good of friends. Chase would come to look for a covey of doves so he could shoot his fool head off. Then he'd brag about how many he killed. Sometimes he'd talk about the peach crop. He's been inside our house one time. I know for a fact Gaten never set foot in his.

Chase Porter didn't say very much. He just looked at Sara Kate and grinned his slow grin. He's got to know he's kind of cute when he grins.

Sara Kate sure was happy he came over. He's been the only one to visit her outside of our kinfolk. Of course I'm not counting people who come to sell stuff. They've been coming ever since the day Gaten died. Yes, people do think when a man dies, he takes his wife's sense to the grave with him. They think Sara Kate hasn't got a bit of sense left over.

Chase Porter is a good catch for any woman. At least that's what Miss Katie says. "Every widow, old maid, and young girl in Round Hill has tried to get him. Even some married ones," she laughed.

I know that Chase Porter ain't hardly got all that money he makes out to have. True, he stands to get all that money his daddy's got when he dies, but old man Porter isn't dead yet.

I like Chase all right and enough. It's his daughter I can't stand. She thinks she's too much for me with her fat spoiled self. She is only ten years old and is as big as a house.

The way her daddy keeps looking at Sara Kate has gotten me to thinking. Just maybe her daddy is trying to court Sara Kate. If they get married, his daughter is dead meat if they try to hang around here.

Chase is wearing light blue jeans, a light blue dress shirt, open at the collar, and a pair of cool shades. I guess he's got on his dress-up boots on account of it being Sunday.

"You didn't happen to see my horse around here, did you, Clover?" I shake my head. Chase knows good and well he's not about to let that high-priced horse get loose. That's just an excuse to come see Sara Kate.

In a way, it's good he did come. Sure helps to spruce up Sara Kate. Having to watch him look at her with that sly grin of his makes me feel kind of funny. I don't want him to think I'm scared to stay on my own front porch just because he's there. So I say, "Care for some ice tea?" I got that from my aunt.

I pour two glasses of tea and stick a piece of lemon, all fancy-like, on the side of the glasses. I filled them so full, the tea spilled all over my hands. I had to walk real, real slow. Sara Kate looked at me, but didn't say nothing. She can't stand it when I fill something too full.

Chase is leaning against a post. His hat is kind of pulled down over his eyes. Not to keep the sun out or anything. He just thinks it's sporty, that's all. He looks down the quiet, quiet road. "Seems like everybody is in church except us," he grins. "I won't run the risk of going to church, because if I show up, the Lord might think it's time to bring the world to its end."

A whole week has passed. It's Sunday again. I'll bet you anything, sure as shooting, Chase Porter is going to bring his grinning self over here.

In a way, I guess it's good he comes. At least, all that sadness that balls up in Sara Kate's eyes sometimes will go away. I tell you, a person would have to be blind not to see she likes Chase.

"You should go out more, Sara Kate," Chase tells her. "My aunt says she'd love having you over for tea sometimes." I think to myself, your aunt ought to ask her then.

Sara Kate smiles. "Your cousin, Mary Ellen, promised to invite me to a dinner party."

Chase scratches his head and grins some

more. "She is not likely to ask you, either," he says. "You see, she thinks she's pretty uppity-crusty now. Before she married my cousin, she didn't have two dimes to rub together. The high-and-mighty Mary Ellen once had to work as hard as a damn nigger woman, just to pay her rent."

Sara Kate winced when he said that right before me, and sucked in her breath. The corners of her mouth tightened.

What Chase said brought on a strange quiet. Then after it had a chance to sink in, in a rambling sort of way that made no sense at all, Chase sort of tried to apologize. To try to undo a thing he didn't at first even realize he'd done. Poor old dumb Chase. Now that it had sunk in what he'd said, he was so ashamed. He couldn't even hold his head up. Just kept his eyes fastened on his fancy boots.

For what seemed like a long time Chase kept his head down. Then he raised his eyes and looked to see if Sara Kate had been hurt by the word, nigger.

Sara Kate's face showed she'd heard him all right. Yet her face didn't show anger, just her disappointment in him. Her face just sort of closed down. She didn't choose to make something out of it. She didn't say anything and neither did Chase.

Shame had played, my daddy would have said, "its most magnificent role for Chase Porter."

Any further hurt anyone could have given wasn't necessary. I believe Sara Kate got away with him more than if she had gotten him told.

Daniel said there's a lot more ways to hurt somebody than getting them told. Like using spit for instance.

It's funny, but all this time Daniel and I thought Sara Kate would make a slip someday and say nigger. If she ever did, Daniel said, all I'd have to do is hint that folks spit in stuff people eat or drink if they say nigger. He said you don't have to even do it. If they think you did, they'll vomit the rest of their life.

Daniel couldn't fool me up to do that, though. My daddy and Grandpa would haunt me for the rest of my born days. That's way too nasty to even think of.

I don't think we'll see too much of Mr. Chase Porter with that slow easy grin for a long time.

At least after this Chase thing, I've learned

a thing or two more about Sara Kate. She's not all that good and sweet all the time. She's got her mean streaks, too.

Like sometimes when she thinks Chase Porter is calling her, she will let that telephone almost ring off the hook. She will be sitting right there looking at it and she won't even pick it up.

But you know, it serves Chase right. Looks like with all the stuff you see on TV, Chase should know you can't even say something unkind about black folks today and get away with it. Much less use the word nigger.

Eight

♣ ♣ ♣

Sara Kate has stuff spread all over the kitchen table when I come in from the peach shed.

She glanced up at the wall clock. A worried frown crossed her face. "Oh, dear, I had no idea it was getting so late. I'll clear this away and start lunch. We'll shop for food as soon as we're finished."

"Some of those little pigs in a blanket you have in the freezer would go good," I say, adding, "we can throw some Tater Tots in the microwave, too."

"Oh, all right," Sara Kate said. For a change she didn't say we had to have a vegetable or salad.

I put on water to boil for ice tea. I can't drink the stuff when Sara Kate makes it. She doesn't put a drop of sugar in it. Just puts it into the fridge to get cold, then puts sugar on the table so you can sweeten it. It takes almost the whole bowl of sugar to get the cold stuff sweet.

I look at all the different things Sara Kate has been drawing. "How in the world did you learn to draw like this?" I ask her.

"I've always liked to draw since I was a child," she said, "and then when I was older, I went to school to study design and commercial art. Afterwards I apprenticed for awhile, learning textile design, fabric, wallpaper, and such. And I've been doing it ever since. I am under contract to do designs for several textile mills in the Carolinas. It's nice because I can work at home and send the designs to them."

"I wish I could draw like you," I say.

"I'll make up a box of paints for your very own, and I'll teach you. Right now we better get to the store."

Sara is reading labels in the frozen foods section at the Winn Dixie grocery store. We just left Harris-Teeter's. The music is better over here. Good dancing music is playing.

I try to stand still. I know how much Sara Kate hates it when I dance in the stores. Right now, though, I don't think I'm going to be able to keep from dancing. Everything inside of me is pulling at me, begging me to dance.

I start snapping my fingers. Sara Kate is

looking at me. I look her straight in the eyes and then moon dance down the aisle. I add the new steps Daniel showed me. It's easy on the slick waxed floors.

A gray-haired woman I don't even know breaks into a wide grin when she sees me. And then with her eyeglasses draped on a chain around her neck, a half gallon jug of Clorox in one hand, and a three-pound bag of pinto beans in the other, she dances down the aisle with me.

Sara Kate is watching us, but I don't hardly care. I just go ahead and get d.o.w.n. She has stopped frowning and I sort of believe she wishes she could dance with us.

A large sign in the store says "REGISTER TO WIN A COLOR TELEVISION." The drawing will be held in two weeks. I grab a big, big stack of entry blanks for me and Daniel to fill out. The sign says you must be over eighteen to enter, so we'll put his mama and daddy's name on them.

I see the store manager hurrying towards me. I know he wants me to put them back. I head toward Sara Kate. He is right behind me. Sara Kate is over by the tea and coffee. She picks up a box of Lipton's Blackberry Tea. I touch her on the arm. "I picked these up for you, Sara Kate."

"Thanks, honey." She doesn't even look around.

The store manager turns as red as his red hair. He scratches his head, turns to leave, stops, looks back, then walks away. There is no way he's going to take on Sara Kate Hill. She looks like she's somebody real important.

At the checkout counter Sara Kate lets me buy one bar of candy and one pack of sugar-free bubble gum. The checkout clerk looks at me, then at Sara Kate. Her long brown hair hangs in dirty ropes. Most of the clerks have their hair frizzed just like us when we get a curl. Some look like a bush, but most wear a controlled frizzy. I can't picture Sara Kate wearing any kind of frizz.

The clerk turns the Lipton tea boxes over. I can tell by her eyes she's never had peach and blackberry tea before. I haven't, either.

Sara Kate tells me to run back and get ice cream. She doesn't tell me to put any back when I bring peach, vanilla, and strawberry. I never buy chocolate. Gaten and I never liked it. We liked milk chocolate candy, though.

It's a good day to buy ice cream. It's not the third of the month when the Social Security checks come or the time for whatever check comes on the first. Best of all, the woman in front of us didn't have to write a check and turn in a thousand coupons. She did hunt in her pocketbook for a penny until Sara Kate gave her one.

The clerk blows and shrugs her shoulder when Sara Kate whispers she may not have enough money. I imagine she thinks if you can afford to buy all that high-priced stuff you ought to have plenty of money. She has enough. She takes two fifty-dollar bills that look like they've been ironed from a wallet with little tan designs on it.

Sara Kate is passing everything on the road. She is driving Gaten's truck really fast.

It's broad daylight, yet a sleepy possum wanders onto the highway. Sara Kate slams on the brakes so hard a bag of groceries slides off the seat. Her outstretched arm holds me back.

"You're going to mess around and get me killed," I fuss. "And all on account of some old possum. He ain't got no business out here in the first place. He knows he can't see this time of day with his pink eyes."

"I told you to fasten your seat belt, honey." Sara Kate is looking at the opossum. "He must be sick."

134

On the side of the road a dead black snake, turned belly-side up, shines like a silver belt. I'll bet anything that old sick possum was eating on it. You couldn't pay me to eat no possum.

We pass a house where an old woman is plowing through a pile of clothes at a yard sale. Her feet are stuck into a pair of worn fur-lined bedroom shoes. A bright purple garment with splashes of yellow is tucked under her arm. The main thing she seems to need is a pair of shoes.

If Sara Kate hadn't forgotten to buy bird seed, we wouldn't have had to turn right around and go back to Harris-Teeter's the very next day. And we wouldn't have run into Miss Kenyon.

Sara Kate is the only person in Round Hill that buys food for everything that flies or crawls. I can see buying seed for birds in the wintertime. But you're not supposed to feed them in the summer. We head back to the store.

I sure hope Sara Kate won't go buying the fancy dog treats and stuff she did the last time. Gideon staggered up one day all drunk up, and Sara Kate let him go in the kitchen for a glass of water. Well sir, he ate every bit of the dog food on top of the refrigerator. It didn't kill him, though.

When we drove into the parking lot and she parked right beside Miss Kenyon's car, I thought I'd die. If Sara Kate had known how much Miss Kenyon hated her guts for taking Gaten away from her, she'd never have parked there. Sara Kate wouldn't have known it was Miss Kenyon's car in the first place. She's not into cars.

Well, anyway, when we came out of the store, there was Miss Kenyon.

"Hey, Miss Kenyon," I said.

"Why, hey, Clover," she grinned, but swallowed it when she turned to Sara Kate.

"Mrs. Hill."

Sara Kate smiled, "Hi."

"I didn't know you were still in Round Hill," Miss Kenyon lied.

"Oh yes, I'm still around," Sara Kate said, "but I've been very busy."

"I suppose you're busy with your book."

"My book? I don't understand."

Miss Kenyon is almost in Sara Kate's face. "The first thing you people usually do in life is write a book. So I'm sure you've joined all the other white Southern women writers. Eager to grab at the chance to say all the things you would love to say, but afraid to say.

"You want to know how I feel about what most of your kind write? I think, if it's in your mind to write, it's in your head to say." She is stepping on Sara Kate's toes. Her face is as red as a beet.

Miss Kenyon's shopping cart was in the hot sun. Her ice cream was melting. She didn't care. Nothing could stop her. It was like a play on TV.

"If you ever write like the others, even in fiction, that our houses are dirty, our black men are shiftless, and dare use the word nigger, you'd better be prepared to leave Round Hill, South Carolina."

I don't believe Sara Kate knew how to get Miss Kenyon told off. Gaten must have figured she needed looking after. I guess that's why he married her. He would have counted on me to help her out. I couldn't let Gaten down. "Come on, Sara Kate," I said, "we got to get home."

No matter how hard I try, I cannot get this book thing out of my head. Maybe Sara Kate is writing a book about the people in Round Hill. Maybe Daniel found it, and sneaked it out when he couldn't get me to do it.

I think of the way Sara Kate was looking around Miss Katie's house. She sure can't write that the house stinks. As soon as Miss Katie opens her door the smell of air fresheners and scented potpourri hits you. She spends days on end stuffing the strong-scented leaves, wood shavings, and dried flowers into little Ziplock plastic pouches. She gets paid two or three cents a bag. She said she made might near a hundred dollars one month.

Yep, Miss Katie's got junk. But at least you won't see roaches flying and jumping all over the place like bull frogs. I reckon not. Miss Katie's got roach powder in every crack and Ball mason jar lid she can find.

I think now of that day Sara Kate sat there flipping through all Miss Katie's *Vanity Fair* and *Forbes* magazines. Maybe Miss Kenyon was right about Sara Kate marrying my daddy to get into our lives and show us up. Miss Kenyon said we would provide the fodder she needed.

Now if Sara Kate needs a dirty house to write about, she ought to go to Skip Howe's house. Skip is one of my classmates. He is white and lives in one of the dirtiest houses I've ever seen in my whole life.

When Skip got hurt real bad cutting grass,

the teacher picked me to take a fruit basket to him. Talk was that Skip's real hurt was not so much from what the lawn mower did, as what his daddy did to him for borrowing Tom Jenkins's lawn mower. Skip's daddy has been missing ever since the accident. They say his daddy liked to killed him. His mama hushed the whole thing up.

Skip had no business going over to old stingy Tom Jenkins and borrowing his lawn mower in the first place. He knew he didn't know how to use a power lawn mower. To begin with, there is not enough grass to waste your spit on in the red clay yard jammed with old wheelless cars, auto tires, rims, beer cans, and chickens. Nothing can grow. You wonder why they would even want to cut a spot of grass no bigger than a minute. Folks say, Jenkins had no business loaning people as poor as the Howes anything.

Poor Skip. He didn't know not to pull grass out of a lawn mower while it was still running.

I had to pick my steps around dog mess all over the yard, then dodge chicken mess on the front porch. On top of all the dirt inside, Skip's mama was smoking. Smoking and coughing. The fingers on her trembling hand were stained yellow as gold.

The skin on her has so many lines, it looks like chicken scratching. "Them some right pretty things you wearing honey," she said, adding, "especially them shoes." I do have on a pretty dress for a change. I said, "Thank you." I look down at my shoes. My aunt Ruby Helen sent me the dress and shoes.

I guess they do seem kind of fancy for Round Hill. One thing is for sure, Gaten would have never spent that kind of money on clothes. He claimed his money was always tied up in his peaches. "Can't ever guarantee a peach crop, baby," he always said. "Farming is a card game. You're playing dirty pool, but you never get to hold a trump card." Or he might have said ace, I can't remember. I do know he did say, "The weather can call its hand anytime. And in a second, the game is over."

Skip's mama was dressed in dirty pink cutoffs and a sleeveless turquoise polyester blouse. A yellow plastic headband held her hair back. She didn't have a tooth in her mouth. Skip was sick, yet he was dirty as he could be. Talk about poor, they are some kind of poor.

I'm not sure Skip knows it, though. He seemed happy enough snuggled in an old couch with springs popping out everywhere.

An old spread with foam rubber backing was shedding all over the place. He grinned as he read all the names signed on his get-well card.

Skip answered for me when his mama offered food. "Aw, Ma, she don't want nothing to eat." He knew good and well I was not about to eat a bit in that house.

Skip's mama brought him a big plate of pinto beans and white biscuits. She brushed a few strands of bright red hair off his forehead. Skip had a really neat baseball cap turned sideways on his head. That's the style. Like everything they had, it was secondhand.

His mama tried to get him to take off his cap to say his blessing and eat. But he wouldn't do it. His old hateful daddy must have torn up his head. I will bet you anything that even as poor as Skip is, he had some kind of new haircut hid under that cap. I reckon, if you don't have a penny to your name, you still want to look in style. Poor Skip was some kind of ashamed when a big fat roach crawled right into his pinto beans.

Gaten always told me never to look down when someone spoke to me. But I had to look down then. I sure couldn't look at Skip. I was so sorry and ashamed for poor Skip,

I could have died. I didn't care if he was white.

There was a smell in that house that was more than a smell of dirt. It wasn't Skip's hand and arm, all closed up in dirty bandages, either. After Mrs. Howe told me she was eaten up with cancer, the smell filled the room. It swallowed up the smell of everything. Even the loud-smelling pinto beans. It was the smell of death.

I told them I had to go, and split.

Gaten had our supper ready when I got out of the tub. We had skillet cornbread, hot dogs, and beans. Gaten loved him some cornbread. The beans seemed to move on my plate. I couldn't eat a bit. I told Gaten about the roaches and the cancer. He only said, "Now, now, Clover, let's not get carried away." I think of how I could fool Sara Kate into going down to their house to borrow a cup of sugar.

I think of the look that would come over Sara Kate's face if she walked into that house and Skip's mama said, "Have a seat." And I smile.

Nine

♣ ♣ ♣

Whenever I look towards Miss Katie's house now, the first thing I think of is the big prize she won. A boat.

I hope it won't be like the diamond wristwatch she got as a big prize. A black plastic thing with a diamond the size of a speck of sand staring out at you like a piece of broken glass.

The big envelope in our mailbox announcing *You May Be A 10 Million Dollar Winner* is for Miss Katie. The mailman wouldn't keep putting her mail in our box if she stopped making glue out of honey and egg whites. She uses it to glue on all those faded, rain-washed stamps she finds. Her mailbox is so loaded with ants, the mailman hates to stick his hand in it.

"I think *you* ought to take this mail to Miss Katie," I tell Sara Kate when she hands it to me to take. "It will give you a chance to visit. You always said you were going to on account of how good she's been to us since Gaten died. It would be good if you get to know folks in Round Hill better, anyway."

I didn't tell Sara Kate that people were starting talk that she was a stuck-up nasty white so-and-so.

I think to myself that just maybe if Sara Kate goes with me, Miss Katie might show us the boat.

It's almost 12:30 P.M. I can tell without even looking at a clock. Through the still, hot and dry air, the theme song from "The Young and the Restless" blares out. Plunk —plunk. It seems like everybody in our section is hard of hearing.

A speeding dump truck with two wheels on the hard surfaced road, two on the dirt, rounds the curve. Sara Kate and I part. One on one side, one on the other. The sandy grit stings our faces.

Miss Katie is in her front yard. Her print dress is pulled and puffed up behind by cockleburs. Her white fluffy hair hangs in two plaits. Miss Katie looks as old as her house.

She dry spits specks of tobacco from her tongue and wipes her mouth with the back of her hand. But when she starts to talk, tiny pieces of tobacco fly out like greasy blackberry seeds. "Excuse my yard," she says. "Too hot for somebody my age to keep things up like Clover's daddy used to keep up his place. It's still kept up so good you'd think white folks lived there." She looks at Sara Kate, gives a sick grin and drops her head. Embarrassed!

Sara Kate turns her usual pinkish red. I look down at my feet and kick the ground. I don't know what I'd do with myself sometimes if I didn't have my feet.

Miss Katie waves us in, out of the sun. "A heat stroke can slip up on a person before they know it." She moves slowly, every move studied, thought out, like an old woman. Miss Katie is old. She eases into a rocking chair and fans with a cardboard fan. It has a picture of a little black girl on it. Her hair is fixed like little girls in old TV movies. It's a funeral home fan.

Miss Katie tell us to sit down. But there are no empty chairs. She starts gathering up stuff. There is more magazines and sweepstakes mail than you can shake a stick at. Every letter shows her getting closer and closer to millions of dollars. Every stamp that ordered another magazine changed the prize to even more millions. At least that's what Miss Katie was led to believe.

Gaten once said, "If Miss Katie saved the money she spent on magazines trying to win the sweepstakes, she'd be pretty well-off for an old lady." But my daddy couldn't tell Miss Katie nothing. Nobody can.

Propped on a table crowded with what-nots, artificial flowers, and faded starched crocheted doilies that stand up is a big blue-bordered notice from American Family Publishers that reads in bold print, "THE NIGHT WHEN MRS. KATIE LEE BROWN WON THE WHOLE TEN MILLION DOLLARS!"

Sara Kate's eyes search the rooms. Rooms filled with as much stuff as a Sears & Roebuck catalog. There are store bought ready-made brooms everywhere. They are neatly placed beside homemade ones, made from wild broomstraw gathered from open uncultivated farm land. The sprigs of straw are tightly tied together with strings of brightly colored print cloth.

Sara Kate tilts her head to one side like a rooster eyeing a crawling caterpillar. She studies the straw brooms. I imagine, like me, she's thinking, what on earth would Miss Katie need brooms for? There is no place to sweep. The only place you can even see the floor is in the narrow path that leads from one room to the other. A needle threader in the path shines like a brand new nickel.

Miss Katie tells her how close we are to the end of the world. Someone stole a shovel and hoe right off her front porch. She can't bring stuff like that inside, because she says it's bad luck.

Miss Katie catches me eying some pretty towels. "They right pretty, ain't they, Clover," she says, flashing a wide toothless grin. She brags that the teeth she ordered years and years ago from an almanac are still as good as new. They ought to be. She never wears them. They say nearly every Sunday she cried out in church, "Oh Lord, I come off and left my teeth."

I guess Miss Katie will stop giving me a couple dollars to cut her grass. She says she's started ordering a batch of fancy hand towels from Fingerhut, in case she has to hand someone a little something. She orders more stuff. She'll send something she gets in the mail back for a free gift. Usually it's some old flower. She never reads far enough to see that if she doesn't send the plant back after so many days, then they bill her and keep sending flowers. So Miss Katie's plants keep coming and she keeps paying.

"The Young and the Restless" is still on

TV. "I just have that old thing on," Miss Katie says. "I don't watch that trash. It ain't fit for no Christian." All the time, though, she is stealing quick looks. Moving her head so we don't block her view. She peeps like a crow checking out a watermelon patch. On television, an emergency broadcast signal sounds. . . . "This is an emergency test," the announcer says, "a test of the emergency broadcast system. . . . This concludes the test," he says at the end. Miss Katie shakes her head. "One day, it will be for real," she whispers.

A shaft of sunlight cuts a path across the room where Sara Kate is sitting. Miss Katie wants her to move out of the hot sun, but there is no place for her to go. The sun has zapped the wind's energy. It's as still as the painted pictures hanging on the torn wall-papered walls. A small, squeaking electric fan pushes sheets of hot air into the corners of the room.

Miss Katie's house never changes much, not even at Christmas. She just sets out little baskets of fruits, nuts, and candy on chairs or on her bed. She can't decorate. There's no place to add a single thing.

Miss Katie knocks a big bundle of S&H green stamp books to the floor and sets off a mouse trap. Kah blam! She peeps from under her hooded eyes, "There ain't a rat in this house." Sara Kate is scared to death. "I keep a trap set all the time," she explains. "Some old rat may sneak in here with his nasty self. But he sure won't live long enough to sneak around. They may crawl in, but they don't crawl out."

Miss Katie sure picked a good time to offer us something to eat. Hands that carry out bleeding rats now bring us big plates of fried pies and carrot cake loaded with thick confectioners sugar icing. She spreads a yellow napkin over my lap and plops the plate down on it.

"It's just a little something," she says. "I know how chaps are. They always want a bite of something sweet." She turned to Sara Kate. "I'll let you help yourself. I'm so glad you're here. Maybe for once Clover will eat something here. Always wants to carry it home. That's not polite, is it, Miss Sara Kate?"

Sara Kate's eyes are glued on those greasy pies. Sara Kate don't eat anybody's greasy stuff.

I pick up my pie and look at Sara Kate. She reaches for my plate. "Oh no, young lady, you're going to have to save this for supper." She turned to Miss Katie. "Clover won't eat anything but sweets if she's allowed. Is it all right if I take it home for dessert tonight?"

Miss Katie grins, "Why sure, Miss Sara Kate. Clover is blessed to have a mama like you." Her smile faded. "Her daddy would have been so proud of you. Real proud."

"I'm clean out of new tin foil," she said, smoothing out an old wrinkled piece. I don't say nothing but I know why she is all out of tin foil. She keeps using it all up wrapping them five-dollar bills in it to send to those TV preachers.

"You must come and eat with me sometimes," Miss Katie is saying. "I had my preacher and his wife over a few months back. I made the best barbecued pig feet and tails. They said it was the best something to eat they'd had in a long time."

Sara Kate doesn't say she knows about pig feet. She'd watched Baby Joe eat plate after plate of them at the family gathering before she married Gaten. I still believe it was the sight of all that grease that made her sick.

Miss Katie shows Sara Kate a pickup notice she got for a television. She comes back to our house to use the phone. I dial the 1-800 phone number for her. She speaks

150

really strong. "I don't have no way to get down there for my TV," she says. "You see, I don't have no car to get way down near Hilton Head, South Carolina. I have a hard time just finding somebody to carry me to the store. I don't reckon you could send it to me, could you?"

We don't know what they said to her. But she said, "Well, thank you anyhow for picking me as the winner."

Poor Miss Katie is really sad. She digs in her apron pocket for some change and tries and tries to pay Sara Kate for a toll-free call.

I think Miss Katie knows she was fooled this time. She seems tired and slowly rocks her body in a straight chair that does not move. Her arms are folded, her mouth chewing away at nothing but empty space. She swallows the empty air. Her lips quietly smack, like a box turtle eating lettuce.

Sara Kate is hurting, too. She sucks in her breath, short and quick. Her body makes little jerks like a child trying to stop crying. If she is not careful and keeps on holding all that hurt in, she's going to start working her mouth, licking her lips and making them quiet sounds like an old woman again.

We stayed around Miss Katie a long, long time. And she didn't breathe word one about

151

her boat. What they all say is true. "Miss Katie sure won't talk about her boat."

If you think the diamond wristwatch she won was bad, you should have been there the day the UPS truck delivered the boat. It was a really big package. They say it will blow up into a big boat like a life raft. I know Miss Katie didn't expect that. The boat wouldn't have been so bad but she had to pay a big delivery charge on top of all the money she sent to them every time she sent back the easy puzzles she solved.

I might be wrong but I believe if Miss Katie had put all that money together she could have bought her a real boat to fish in.

They say when two people live together, they start to look alike. Well, Sara Kate and I have been living together for a long time and there is no way we will ever look alike.

But in strange little ways, we are starting to kind of act alike. Things like the way she helped me out with the fried pies at Miss Katie's house. And little by little, a part of me is slowly beginning to change towards Sara Kate. Even the picture of her face that shed no tears at my daddy's funeral looks different in my mind now. Maybe it's because now I know it wasn't that Sara Kate didn't cry because she didn't care. She didn't because she couldn't.

The truth is, and it's not just because Daniel says so, Sara Kate is strange. Mighty strange sometimes. Like the time I brought her some peaches. "Oh, Clover, you're so good. I love peaches." She just carried on till I said, "You know something, Sara Kate, it wouldn't hurt you one bit to come up to that peach shed for some peaches."

You won't believe this, but her eyes lit up and she thanked me for asking her. Imagine that. Thanking somebody for something that's part theirs in the first place! On second thought, maybe she's a little scared of Everleen.

Anyway, things are shaping up pretty good between us. She doesn't get so mad anymore when I speak my mind. Everleen gets ticked off, though, if I say Sara Kate is changing towards me. She and Miss Kenyon still can't stand her.

Once when I told Everleen how Sara Kate was cleaning up everything so good, she grunted and turned her head. I could see she'd narrowed her eyes to a thin slit and was studying the fence-locust trees, lively and green in spite of the drought. Having those trees means you've got good underground water on your land. At least that's what she says.

Finally she said, "Sometimes a new broom sweeps too clean. Almost all the old family pictures except Gaten's have been swept away." Everleen is right about the pictures. It makes me a little sad that Sara Kate put them in a closet. I think I'll ask her to put them back. Other than that, the new broom can stay like it is. I'm glad Sara Kate won't make me make up my bed and clean up like Gaten used to.

Everleen is busy brushing fuzz off the peaches. "As slow as they are selling we won't need any more today," she says.

"If we do," Daniel complains, "Clover will have to carry the baskets. I've been doing her share of work nearly all month."

Aunt Everleen turned to me, "What is that stepmama of yours doing, Clover? Sitting around drawing those flower designs and such, I guess."

I didn't say anything. I really didn't have to. My aunt nearly always answers her own questions. She moved her chair into a shady spot. "Lord knows I can't see how Sara Kate makes any money at something that piddling. But I reckon she does. Jim Ed offered her some money from what we've been taking in from the peach crop. She said, 'Thanks very much, but right now we are solvent.' One thing we can give the woman credit for, she doesn't back down from providing for you, Clover. Folks say, she stands to get a right good settlement from the accident. Thank the Lord the man had good insurance."

Everleen frowned, "Come to think of it, Sara Kate hasn't breathed a word about it to me." She fanned away bees. "I just remembered, Sara Kate sent word that she wanted to see me. She will probably tell me how much . . ."

Everleen doesn't finish. Just spreads out whatever she's thinking like peanut butter on a slice of bread leaving it there for you to select the kind of jelly needed to finish her thoughts.

Daniel is carving away on a block of wood with his daddy's sharp hunting knife. "Daniel," I warn, "you better stop fooling with that knife. If you mess around and cut yourself you're in real trouble. Sara Kate's not here to put on a tourniquet like she did when you gashed your hand before."

Aunt Everleen bristled up like a bantam rooster. "Daniel doesn't have a mamma to take care of him? No mama standing right here. Right before his face. Who ended up carrying him to the doctor for his stitches anyhow? If you chaps think I can't take care of you, maybe you both should just up and go live with Miss Sara Kate since she is such a first aid expert."

Everleen drew a long breath and sort of rolled her tongue in her mouth. She needed to spread on a little more hurt. "At least I won't have to worry about cooking for the two of you," she said. "I won't have to bake my good cakes or make my good homemade ice cream."

I can see Aunt Everleen is a little peeved with me. I guess I sort of picked the wrong time to brag on Sara Kate. Especially since Daniel and I are wearing the new shades Sara Kate bought us. I have to tell you they were the prettiest shades I've ever seen.

Through the tinted glasses the hot, bright, cloudless sky turns into a cool topaz-colored bowl. Without the shades an airplane streaking across looks like a lump of silver. With my shades on it turns into a lump of topaz floating in a topaz sky.

Aunt Everleen had not seemed too happy the day we got the shades and I sure don't want to stir up more trouble now.

I go over to her and say, "Oh, Aunt Everleen, if you stop cooking darkness will
cover the earth. Our world will look just like
this . . ." I put my shades on her and step
back. "Aunt Everleen," I say, "you look
some kind of cool. Real cool."

Ten

♣ ♣ ♣

Chase Porter cruises along the highway in his brand new pickup. He blows his horn and throws up a hand. We wave back.

"There goes real money," Aunt Everleen says.

"He is sure getting friendly," my uncle puts in. "Hardly a day passes that he doesn't stop by."

Everleen rolls her eyes skyward, "Believe me, it's not on account of us. Chase thinks just by chance the pretty new widow might happen to be here. I could tell by the way he was feasting his eyes on her at the wake it wasn't going to take long for him to start really looking at her. Mourning for them is short. He'll probably be going after her soon." I think to myself, you don't know it, but he already has.

A carload of tired women wearing plastic shower caps stop by the peach shed. They have finished the first shift at the textile mill.

The shower caps keep the cotton out of their perms and greasy Jheri-curls. I'll bet the stores that sell the shower caps make a lot of bucks.

They buy peaches and say they have to hurry on. One of the women had had a wisdom tooth pulled when a zodiac sign was in the head. Because of the mistake she claimed she was in *some* kind of pain.

Everleen laughed, "Girl, once I would have called you backwoods backward. But now I guess you are kind of stylish high class. Maybe even getting on the level with the higher-up women since some of them look to the stars and signs for guidance. They may all do that for all we know." Everleen laughed a nose giggle. "Maybe we ought to get Miss Sara Kate a *Farmer's Almanac*."

Now I don't believe for a minute it would make a speck of difference to Sara Kate where the sign was if she needed to plant something or have a tooth pulled. But then again it just might. It's surprising here of late to learn about the weird stuff that some of them actually believe in.

When they leave, my uncle and aunt go back to the Chase Porter business. They are riding high on their seesaw again. If Everleen says something good about Sara Kate, Jim

159

Ed pulls her right back down to Mudville. She does the same to him when it's her turn.

"Sara Kate won't do too bad if she bags a rich cat like Chase. I still can't get the fancy lizard boots he wore to Gaten's wake out of my mind," Everleen said.

Jim Ed looked at the acres of land stretching beyond the peach orchards. "I don't know if it's the widow or this land Chase has his eye on. You know he'd stand a chance to get a portion of it if he married Sara Kate." Money is raising its ugly head for Jim Ed. You can tell when it touches his sore spot, he becomes bitter.

Everleen grunted, "I can't see that as his reason. Chase has plenty of land and will come into even more, plus money when his daddy's gone. He'll have more land and money than he'll ever need."

Jim Ed breathed a heavy sigh and shook his head. "A white man *never* gets enough land or money."

They have forgotten about some of the good stuff Chase has done. Right off hand, I really can't think of a single soul in all of Round Hill who doesn't think a lot of Chase Porter. Many times he will just up and do a good deed for someone and never let it be known that he was the person who did it. It never mattered if they were white or black.

For instance, one year a late spring freeze killed nearly everyone's peaches except his, and some peach growers down in low country. Poor Miss Annie Grace, with her old half-blind eyes, believed she had peaches in her half-acre orchard. And when she tried to bargain with Chase Porter to sell him her peaches, he didn't have the heart to tell her she didn't have peach one.

You see, there is a vine that often times grows in peach orchards, entwined into peach trees. It's that vine that tripped up my uncle Jim Ed. It's called the trumpet vine or the trumpet honeysuckle. Well, it has these bright red-orange blossoms. It blooms around the time peaches get ripe. Anyway, Miss Annie Grace saw those blossoms in a good many trees and she thought she had peaches. Those blossoms will fool you even when you have good eyesight, much less when you can't half see to begin with.

Miss Annie Grace hopped up and sold Chase Porter her peach crop right over the telephone. Soft-hearted Chase bought her nonexistent peaches. All she wanted for the peaches, since she thought there were not that many, was for Chase to do some tractor work for her. She traded for him to disc her orchard at summer's end and send his hands in the spring to disc, prune, and spray her peaches.

What knocked everybody for a loop was seeing a small trailer full of peaches pulling out of Miss Annie Grace's orchard. What had really happened was Chase Porter's hired hands had slipped the peaches, his peaches, into her orchard. Gaten and Jim Ed couldn't even have pulled it off if they'd wanted to. The peach shed was closed. They had no peaches.

Only someone like Chase Porter would have done such a thing like that anyway. He is known for doing unusual things. Anybody can see why you won't hardly find anybody in Round Hill that will speak hard of Chase.

For some school paper, my daddy once wrote, "Between farmers, there is that communality of souls. In their own special way, farmers have a unique form of religion. All are at times forced to share common experiences and hardships. Together, with usually the same reverence and respect, they bow to the weather for the outcome of their crops . . ."

I can't seem to get Sara Kate and Chase out of my mind. I guess I won't be too bent out of shape if Sara Kate takes up with Chase again. Lord knows he's trying hard enough to get her back.

I have to realize that Chase Porter is really not so bad as he seemed to be the day he messed up with the nigger word. He showed after he'd said it that he knew better. I guess he just plain forgot. Most everybody, young and old, can't remember nothing anymore. Miss Katie said she believes the microwave ovens are cooking our brain cells.

I'm beginning to see I have to speak out for Sara Kate. My aunt and uncle simply can't go on always putting the woman down. "Sara Kate is lonely," I put in for her. "Terribly lonely." The words barely leave my lips before Everleen shoots them down. "Well, look whose side our own little Clover is taking."

Yes, I am taking Sara Kate's side right now. But they can't seem to understand that just because I am, it still doesn't mean I am turning against them. Why can't they see that when you live with someone and they aren't mean or nothing they kind of grow on you?

So, I say to them, "You guys don't have to live and eat with Sara Kate every day of your life and have to watch all the sadness and loneliness that wells up inside her. And you don't have to get embarrassed and all because she does, if she happens not to be able to keep from crying in front of me."

Just thinking about it makes me start to cry. "Oh, little honey," Aunt Everleen says all sugary-like. She looks at Jim Ed and gives him one of her unspoken speeches. Not quite charades. Her body doesn't move, only her eyes. I guess you could call it eye-speak.

She pulls the words from her mouth and puts them into her eyes. They tell Jim Ed to back off Sara Kate, at least in front of me.

Since my aunt and uncle still get a little up-tight about Sara Kate I decide to stop telling them some things that happen at our house. But I think I better tell Aunt Everleen how the plastic flowers got off Gaten's grave. She and Miss Katie were about to open up a full-fledged investigation.

Miss Katie had stormed up to the peach shed after she discovered the brand new plastic flowers she put on Gaten's grave were gone. She was having a living fit. "Go call the police, Everleen," she pleaded. "Go call them. Anybody low-down and dirty enough to stoop to touching something on a dead man's grave need to have the law put on them. It would be beneath me to even spit on the ground where they've stepped."

Aunt Everleen was all set to track down whoever stole the flowers.

All I could think of was someone might have seen me and Sara Kate in the graveyard that early evening.

"Sara Kate," I said, after I told her what was going on, "I think you're in trouble. I think I ought to tell Everleen." She agreed.

Come to think of it we wouldn't have even gone to the graveyard that day if the man that made Gaten's tombstone hadn't called to say he'd placed it on Gaten's grave. He insisted that Sara Kate go check it out to make sure everything was all right. He said he'd been able to get the finest marble found in the state of Georgia. Probably trying to make a big thing over it so she wouldn't be blown away by the bill.

Otherwise, I honestly don't think the woman would have gone to Gaten's grave. Sara Kate is not a graveyard visitor. I hardly think she would have bothered getting a tombstone when she did if Jim Ed hadn't kept hinting he was going to have to break down and buy one himself.

Well, anyway, there we were in the grave-yard. It was after sunset but not yet dark. I stayed inside the truck. You don't catch me fooling around in a graveyard if it's broad daylight and surely not if darkness is about to sweep in.

Gaten's grave was a pathetic sight. Sun-faded plastic flowers from Family Dollar, K-Mart, or yard sales in mayonnaise jars wedged into the earth. If it had been closer to a Sunday the dried-up real flowers would still have been fresh. Sometimes people picked a fresh bouquet from their yard.

Sara Kate was snatching everything off and cramming it into a green plastic bag.

I know Sara Kate is very proper and truly smart. Real smart. If people around here could see the stuff she draws they wouldn't believe she makes up all that fancy stuff right in her head. They would declare she copied them from someone somewhere. Even so, there are things she doesn't know.

Like, for instance, among our people in Round Hill you don't go asking a widow if she likes the kind of flowers you want to put on her dead husband's grave. You just do it.

The dead belong to all to remember. I can only hope and pray that no one saw us there.

I wasn't able to sort out Everleen's true feelings when I told her Sara Kate took the plastic flowers. I stopped short of telling her she threw them away.

When Sara Kate told Everleen she'd made a dreadful mistake, Everleen said, "Repent, sinner and go thy way, and sin no more." Although she smiled it didn't make her words less serious.

Eleven

♣ ♣ ♣

As soon as I hear Sara Kate thank Everleen
for coming, I know I'd better stick around
for awhile. Sara Kate had asked her to come.
I've got to find out why. So I hide and listen.
I have so many secret places in this house,
it's pitiful.

Sara Kate is not one to beat around the
bush. Before she even offers Everleen some
ice tea, she just up and says, "I want to talk
with you about Clover. I hope you have some
free time."

Everleen laughs. "Today, for a change, I
do have time. They poked fun at my supper
last night. So that husband and son of mine
won't get a bite to eat from me tonight. And
they won't eat Kentucky Fried Chicken either unless they walk." She jangled a set of
keys, and laughed some more.

"They sure can't go to my mama's house
looking for something good to eat. Not on a
Thursday night. Mama is so hooked on "The

Cosby Show," she won't even cook for my daddy. He hasn't had a decent meal on Thursday night since the show started.

"Oh my goodness," gracious," she gasps. "Will you listen at me. Running off at the mouth a mile a minute. You were the one who wanted to talk."

Sara Kate sounds upset. "I'm so worried about Clover, Everleen."

"She's not down sick or nothing, is she?" The words rush out Everleen's mouth.

"Oh, no, no," Sara Kate answers hurriedly. "It's just that Clover is too troubled for a ten-year-old child. She's holding in too many thoughts about her father. Here of late, she refuses to even say his name. And if I mention him she immediately clams up."

You're right about that, Miss Sara Kate, I think to myself. I used to talk about Gaten all the time, until she started correcting every little thing I said, and kept telling me to stop talking to myself.

But, you see, when Gaten was busy working on his computer or something, he'd tell me to play his turn at tic-tac-toe. My left hand would be Gaten, my right—me. I used to beat him all the time. I still do. That's how come when I'm playing by myself sometimes, Sara Kate will hear me say,

"Your turn, Gaten. . . . I beat you again, Gaten . . ."

Maybe some of the things I do make Sara Kate think I'm as crazy as Cousin California. Like the game, Killing my Shadow, for instance. It is a little crazy, I guess. You play in the hot sun. Trying to step on a shadow that moves every time you move. You can kill the shadow if you step on the head. And you can only do that at twelve o'clock sharp on most summer days. I guess I am too old to play it, but my grandpa taught me that game.

But you know, I do have sense enough to speak of how my father was, instead of how he is. I do know the past tense from the present and future. I'm not all that dumb.

But come to think of it, I'm not all that smart, either. Lots of times, I get my tenses all mixed up. To tell you the truth, this thing about my high IQ is not exactly right. Deep down I think I've fooled them all. Especially Everleen. She truly thinks I'm so smart I'm gonna make it to Washington, D.C., and out-spell everyone in that spelling bee.

Like I said before, Sara Kate is not letting up on this thing.

"There is also this leg thing, Everleen," she says. "It worries me sick to see her limp.

170

Perhaps it's how it happens. Clover will walk normally for days on end. And then, for no apparent reason, start to limp."

There is dead silence. I know Everleen is thinking. Remember, she's been on me about that limp, too.

Sara Kate finally offers ice tea and cookies. I don't have to see them to know she will get out those fancy paper doilies and those fancy, high-priced cookies that don't taste worth a dime. That woman can spend more in a grocery store than anybody I've ever seen in my life. And we still never have anything good to eat.

Everleen has finally thought this thing out. "You know, Sara Kate, little girls grow into womanhood earlier now than they used to. And their bodies start to change. I was thirteen before my body changed over. Now that could be why Clover's leg aches her. To tell you the truth, Sara Kate, I been planning to talk to Clover, about, about, well, you know what, but I didn't. I figured with you being her stepmother and all, it was sort of your place to tell her."

Everleen knows good and well she's not telling the whole truth. She's been trying to get up enough nerve to tell me ever since we got to the M's in the dictionary. Neither one of them need to tell me. It already happened to my friend, Nairobi, when she was only nine years old. I know, because she told me. I don't care if it never starts for me.

"I can only hope, Everlee" Sara Kate is saying, "that all of this is not only in her mind. There is also this fixation that Clover has about her mother. She really thinks she can remember the things she did. Even the kind of clothes she wore."

"Sometimes the good Lord gives visions," Everleen says quietly. My aunt can face up to anybody in this world. She never gets tongue-tied. If she is pushed into a corner, she'll survive. She will simply put the entire matter into the hands of the Lord. Grandpa always said, "It's hard to buck up against Him." It's now another round for them.

"Let's be reasonable, Everleen. Clover does not remember her mother and it's not healthy for her to believe that she does." Sara Kate's voice is firm. "I do believe that she needs medical attention. And if it's found that there is nothing wrong with her leg, then we'll know it's only in her . . ." Sara Kate stops short. She doesn't have to finish, Everleen knows what she was going to say.

Now if you know about all them half-crazy people in Everleen's family, you know good and well, the slightest hint that somebody in her family, like me, might have something wrong with their mind is going to set her off. Set her off like a match lit under a firecracker. Nobody is going to tell her she's got crazy kin.

I know my aunt is getting cross-eyed and her mouth growing out like Pinocchio's nose. That red hot temper inside her will heat up her skin like it's been microwaved. And her face will start to look all wet and greasy. She is some kind of mad then.

"What you trying to say in a nice fancy way is, the child ain't got right good sense. I don't go for some outsider coming in and trying to cook up that kind of mess." Everleen is getting loud. She starts talking loud and flat when she's mad.

I guess Sara Kate would have had me at some kind of doctor a long time ago if she knew what was really going on in my head all the time. I know for a fact what's wrong with my leg. I hurt it. Hurt it, trying to find my daddy. I was in the backyard feeding the dog when I thought for sure I heard Gaten call me. I ran to the tractor shed. Then my mind told me to check out the woods. I fell over a log and almost broke my leg, but I didn't find Gaten.

That old empty hammock in the yard bothers me a lot, too. Nobody, but nobody, ever uses it any more. It seems to still hold only the imprint of my daddy's figure.

I've never told anybody I even hurt my leg. And I sure will never tell that my leg seems to hurt more whenever I think about Gaten. I guess in a way I'm still thinking I'm just having a bad, bad dream and I'll wake up and see Gaten standing there.

Sara Kate said I keep getting those sharp pains in my eyes because I shift them so sharply and I'm always rolling my eyes. I keep cutting my eyes so sharp because sometimes it seems like I catch a glimpse of my daddy. I can understand all of that. It's what's going on in my head that worries me.

My daddy's funeral was a long time ago, but sometimes I can still hear the singing, children singing without music. Singing along with Miss Kenyon. Only Miss Kenyon wasn't singing at all. She was only opening her mouth and moving her lips. Like Aunt Ruby Helen, sadness had swallowed up her voice. The singing is sad and sounds faraway like the sound of echoes bouncing across hills.

I think of the hearse that brought my daddy's body to our house for a last good-bye.

In my head, the sound of the funeral cars start and stop, but it takes a long time for the singing to stop. The funeral program called the singing accappella or something.

The singing seems so real. The wake still seems pretty real in my head, too. The soft, soft music playing so quietly you could have heard a pin drop.

The crowds of people that filed by the open casket cast silent looks, and with noise-less footsteps made silent exits.

"Mama, mama," a little girl whispered really loud. "Hush," her mama whispered back equally as loud. "Is this what they call a wake?" the little girl whispered again.

A young woman in real tight pants and spike heel shoes made a quiet entrance and stood looking down at Gaten for a long, long time. "That's Minnie Faye Baker's daughter," someone whispered. "She's right nice-looking," someone whispered back. Outside a group of happy children played handball against the brick wall. Kuh thump, kuh thump.

The whispering, a few soft coughs, and many, many soft sad sobs were the only sounds that punctured the soft strange music.

I didn't know half the people who were

there. After about thirty minutes they ushered us to waiting cars. The wake was over. The next day the funeral was held, then like the wake it was over. Yet it's all still left in my head. Sadness still floating about like heavy rain clouds. I don't like death one single bit.

I wonder, when will I become too old to stop remembering all that stuff? Maybe next year.

In the kitchen, Everleen is moaning and carrying on. "Lord, Lord, if Gaten Hill had even the slightest notion somebody was thinking there was something the matter with his baby child's mind, he'd turn over in his grave. He was proud of that baby girl of his. Lord, was he some kind of proud." She sounds like she's going to cry. But she's not. She never cries unless somebody, anybody, dies.

But Sara Kate cries. "I'm sorry. So very sorry," she whispers over and over.

Except for the crying, it's quiet for a long time in the kitchen.

Everleen finally speaks. "Clover's head is all right, Sara Kate. It's in better shape than ours. If that child limps, it's because of grief and sorrow. The child can't shake her sorrow. Just a few years apart she lost her grandpa and her daddy. The poor child ain't even got no mama. Don't you understand that or do you people have no feelings for your lost loved ones?"

Sara Kate draws a sharp breath. "I don't believe I've given you any reason to say that, Everleen. Remember, I lost Gaten, too. But it's Clover we're concerned with, and I am her mama now."

Everleen must know she has gone too far. Her voice becomes soft and kind. "There is nothing wrong with our little Clover, Sara Kate. She is depressed, that's all. We can cure all that with just a little time and a whole bunch of love."

"Perhaps you're right, Everleen. But I still think we should both keep an eye on Clover."

After supper, Sara Kate and I watch television for a little while. On the coffee table is a book about girls growing up. Sara Kate has opened it to a subject on puberty. She doesn't want to be the one to have to tell me. I guess nobody wants to take on that burden. They always want to give it to someone else. I guess it's kind of good I won't have to put that burden on my daddy now. A few days later, on my bed I find a brand new little white bra and a rag doll. It seems

Sara Kate knows I'm starting to grow up but yet she wants me to stay a little girl.

I do believe the leg business being in my mind is settled now. Sara Kate hasn't mentioned taking me to the doctor again. Sometimes when I'm playing, she will tell me not to hurt myself.

The only sad part is, it's only settled with Sara Kate and my aunt. The truth is my leg really hurts a lot of the time. Right now it's hurting.

Maybe Everleen is right. The heavy load of pain and sadness is too much for my mind and soul. So my leg is helping them out.

Twelve

♣ ♣ ♣

I still think back on the day I got into real serious trouble with Sara Kate. It was, after all, partially her fault to begin with. She had no business making me come all the way home every day for lunch. Even if Jim Ed or Gideon did drive me. I've always been plenty satisfied eating Everleen's cooking.

At first coming home was great. If I didn't like the fancy lunches she made, Sara Kate would let me fill up on whatever I wanted, ice cream, cookies, or snacks.

Afterwards, sometimes we would sit on the front porch for awhile. Sometimes we talked. Mostly we didn't, though. It's still kind of hard getting used to someone like Sara Kate. She just doesn't seem to fit in anyplace. For instance, for the length of time she has been here, the only company she's had outside of Gaten's people are people trying to sell something. I'll bet she has had a dozen insurance and Avon people here.

That particular day had started out bad. Sara Kate was in a terrible mood. She watched me play with my lunch. It was pretty enough, real fancy and all, but I sure didn't want to eat it. The day of the good old ice cream lunch is now history.

"Do you want to freshen up and change your clothes before you go back, Clover?" Sara Kate asked me. She kills me, always asking if I want to do something, instead of just up and telling me what she wants me to do. She knows she wants me to take off my dirty jeans and tee shirt.

"Sara Kate," I say, "looks like common sense ought to tell you not to keep on asking me if I want to do this or that. You should know good and well that I am going to say no. Strange, you didn't ask me if I wanted this nasty lunch."

She gave me a hard cold look. "Clover, I've been working really hard all morning. Yet I stopped in the middle of everything to make your lunch. It happens to be a very good one. But even if it isn't, you have got to learn to be appreciative, young lady. I happen to have feelings like anyone else."

I turned my head away, thinking to myself what she said about working so hard. It blows me away that she calls sitting down in a cool air-conditioned house, drawing and painting designs, hard work. What my aunt Everleen does is hard work, picking peaches in the hot sun, and then hanging around that hot peach shed all day trying to sell them.

Sara Kate is still eyeing me. "I suggest you eat your lunch, young lady."

Well, when I told Sara Kate she could take her lunch and shove it, she really flew off the handle. She sort of lost it. "You apologize this minute, Clover Hill," she screamed. Her face turned a bright red. Her eyes blazed.

To tell you the truth, I cannot believe I actually said what I did. I have never said anything like that before. It's truly too bad to repeat. I would have never said anything like that to Gaten. I started backing out of the door, but she stopped me.

One thing for sure, I am not afraid of the woman. Never was, never will be. There is no way anybody can be afraid of someone who is too kind-hearted to even kill a little gnat.

"Thank you very much for lunch, Miss Sara Kate," I said and ran from the house.

Sara Kate followed right behind me in the truck. When she got there, you could tell she had been crying. "Everleen," she said weakly, "we've got to talk."

I can tell you, it's not a good feeling to know that you've made a grown woman cry.

They talked all right. Sara Kate told everything that happened between us. Exactly the way it happened. She even told her exactly what I'd said.

Even as bad as it all was, I still find it kind of hard to believe that Everleen took Sara Kate's side. But I guess what's right is right. Everleen was as mad as a stinging bumblebee. "That's no way to behave, Clover Lee Hill, it's unbecoming to you," she told me. "I've been letting you get out of hand here of late. You are not a grown woman, even if you do think you are. You have no excuse for acting that way. It would be different if the woman was treating you like a dog or something.

"Now you just put in your head that you are a child. And as a child you've got to learn that many times older people know what is best for you. Whew," she blew. I guess she had fussed out. She crossed her arms in front of her. "Now you tell Sara Kate you are sorry for the way you acted."

For a long time, I just stood there. I studied Everleen's face, searching for some sign, any little thing, maybe just a slight wink, something to let me know it was just a front she was putting on to keep peace in the family. I needed a sign to let me know she was on my side. But there was no sign.

Everleen did not take her eyes from my face. She moved her hands and planted them firmly on her hips. "I am waiting on you, Clover," she said, "but I sure don't plan to stand here and wait forever."

I dropped my head. I couldn't stand to look at either one of them. I was so glad Daniel was with his daddy, I didn't know what to do. I would have been so ashamed if he'd been there.

Finally I said, "I apologize, Sara Kate. I'm sorry for the way I acted." But then under my breath I said, ever so softly, "But you shouldn't have tried to make me eat the lunch." And dag, they both heard it.

Everleen's voice had softened, "Try to look over her little fast cutting remarks, Sara Kate. She really didn't mean any harm with that last remark. The poor little thing has just not been herself here of late.

"You see, Sara Kate, sometimes the child has to hear more around this peach shed than I'd like. I wish I didn't have to keep the kids here. Every bad word that's used sticks to their brain like a suction cup. But Lord knows, I don't know what I would do without them."

Sara Kate smiled at Everleen. "Oh, I'm beginning to learn how to handle things like that. I treat those kind of sayings, coming from a small child, like small fish. You simply toss them back into the water."

I can clearly see that Sara Kate is no longer angry with me. And it gives me a good feeling. I think just having Everleen not dump on her, plus take her side, did her all the good in the world.

Maybe Sara Kate became so happy after her talk with Everleen because she knew she was planning to clamp down tight on me. Now I imagine she believes Everleen will side with her if I get the least bit out of line.

For a few days, I have halfway been thinking that, just maybe, I will tell Sara Kate about my leg. "Sara Kate," I've made up my mind to say, "I was just thinking that, maybe, well, maybe you should take me to see that old doctor about my leg."

As usual, like with everything else, I didn't do it. I sure didn't plan for things to turn out the way they did yesterday.

Like always, I was home for lunch. It was

not too bad for a change. Hamburgers on crusty seed-topped buns with pink juice running out the meat. I'm getting so I like them that way, now. Sara Kate gave me a small dish of pork-n-beans, and of course a salad. She always makes salads. She didn't eat any of the beans. She seldom does.

When we finished, she put a small plate of cookies on the table. Can you believe that just for the two of us, no company or nothing, she put a lacy paper doily under the cookies.

Well, anyway, you know that funny feeling your mouth gets when you are eating, and your mind keeps telling you, you still have half of a cookie or something left to eat. Yet you can't find it anyplace.

It's hard to explain that feeling, but the thing itself is very, very real. That was in my mind, so I was looking everywhere, all around my plate, under my napkin.

"What are you looking for, Clover?" Sara Kate asked.

"Nothing," I said. I was looking for something and she knew it. I wouldn't say what it was, because it was too hard to put into words why I was looking so hard for half of a butter creme cookie.

I must have twisted my leg or something

185

when I got ready to leave, because the thing started hurting me so bad, I couldn't help myself. I started crying like a newborn baby.

Sara Kate rushed behind me. Her eyes wide. "It's your leg, isn't it, Clover?"

Like I said, I wasn't ready for her to find out. Daniel and I were supposed to go fishing. Daniel was right when he said you can't hide anything from her.

"How in the world do you think my leg can keep from hurting, Sara Kate? I have to run and carry peach baskets every morning." I was still crying. "So what if it's hurting, it is my leg, you know." I had promised myself to stop being a smart aleck, but that just slipped out.

Sara Kate didn't get angry. "Let's get dressed, Clover," she said, "we are going to the doctor."

You guessed it. I wound up in the doctor's office.

The doctor was quick to see I was not about to say anything about my leg. So he started tapping, pressing, and feeling my leg. He finally said I must have injured the leg somehow. He sure didn't get it out of me first, though. I might even have kept him from finding out that I'd hurt it. The trouble was I couldn't help but say "ouch" when he pressed down too hard in one place.

I thought of the time, not too long ago, when Mr. Elijah Watson hurt his leg. They said gangrene set in. And you know what, they put him in the hospital and cut the dang leg clean off. See, Sara Kate doesn't even know stuff like that.

I decided on my own to tell the doctor I fell over a log and hurt my leg. He wanted to take X-rays of my leg. I've never had one before. They may hurt for all I know. Well, telling him what happened sure didn't help. I had to have the thing X-rayed anyway.

The doctor pointed out shadowy areas on the X-ray to Sara Kate. "There is no damage to the bones," he said. "Your daughter likely tore a ligament in the beginning and doubtless kept hurting the same leg over and over." He called me her daughter. Sara Kate had called me her daughter. She kept saying it. The only time she said Clover was when she spoke to me. Now that was really something.

I guess my leg wasn't really hurt all that bad after all. The doctor didn't put bandage one on my leg. I thought if you hurt your leg or something, they ought to bandage it up. They sure did it when Skip caught his arm in the lawn mower. Sure would have saved me from carrying peach baskets if he'd put it in a cast or up in bandages.

Since the doctor didn't make such a big deal over my leg and put me in the hospital, I figured as long as I was there it might be safe to tell him about the poison I got into my eye.

Well, that bolted Sara Kate right out of her seat. She was upset that I hadn't told her about it. She fastened her eyes on me. I do believe her eyes change color when she is angry. They didn't move. It was like they were held in place with scotch tape. "Why didn't you tell me, Clover?" she asked.

I hung my head. "I was afraid you would take me to the doctor," I whispered.

The doctor sat down in front of me, looked under both my eyelids and shined a bright light in my eyes. He said there was no damage to the eyes. But I should always let someone know if I got something in my eyes. He explained that sometimes you need to wash out the eye with special solutions.

I looked up at the doctor. He was smiling. "I won't be afraid next time," I said.

Sara Kate half-smiled. "I should certainly hope not, young lady. Now thank the good doctor and let's get on home."

I must have groaned in my sleep or something, because when I woke up Sara Kate was by my side, tucking the sheets about me. Trying to brush my hair off my forehead. Like it could possibly fall there in the first place. She, of all people, should know that after she messed up my hair with that perm, there is no way it can fall anywhere.

My hair will fall when Aunt Everleen fixes it. She straightens it. One day at school, a little girl with her blue-eyed self had the nerve to ask me if I ironed my hair on an ironing board.

Sara Kate stayed in my room for a long time. I think she was waiting for me to fall asleep. It was a bright moonlit night. I could see her as plain as my hand before my face. She stood by the window staring into the still night.

I could also see the brown marks on the ceiling. Rain marks from a leaky roof. Poor Gaten. He fixed the roof, but didn't live long enough to paint the ceiling. I study the brown splashes and marks. If you let your eyes work on the ceiling for awhile, you can make all kinds of monsters out of them.

The next morning I was up before sunup and already bright orange-colored clouds were spread out in neat rows getting ready for the sun. Right across the doorway was the biggest spider web I'd ever seen. Smack-dab in the middle was a big spider. I was all set to cream the thing, when I thought about Sara Kate. Somehow I just couldn't bring myself to kill it. That was the first time something like that happened to me. Sara Kate's thinking is rubbing off on me for sure.

Come to think of it, Gaten may not have been so keen on killing spiders, either. I remember him telling me the story of Robert the Bruce. He said, according to legend, "Bruce, hiding from enemies in a wretched hut, watched a spider swinging by one of its threads. It was trying to swing itself from one beam to another. Bruce noticed the spider tried six times and failed. The same number of battles he had fought in vain against the English. He decided, if the spider tried a seventh time and succeeded, he also would try again. The spider did try and was successful. So Bruce tried once again and went forth to victory."

I believe I remember every single story Gaten ever told me. That man knew so much stuff, I wonder how his head held it all.

Now as far as killing goes, Sara Kate is

not behind everything I don't kill. I won't kill a snail, for instance. Never have. There was one crawling on the steps right then. Its slow moving body left a nasty slimy trail. But, by dog, I didn't rub him out. I couldn't have stood the squishy mess he would have made. I watched the big spider hurry away, and went in to cook breakfast. A part of me was little by little starting to obey and care for Sara Kate without my even knowing it.

When Sara Kate came into the kitchen, I was standing on the little stool my daddy made for me, stirring a pot of cheese grits. I can solid cook grits. Gaten couldn't stand nobody's lumpy grits. I've been cooking since I was eight years old. Sara Kate made coffee while the ham and canned biscuits finished cooking. I crossed my eyes and watched her double image sip a cup of black coffee. Gaten and I always put canned Pet milk in our coffee.

Sara Kate spread somebody's homemade peach jelly on a buttered biscuit and put it on my plate. "Please don't cross your eyes, Clover."

When she is ready to eat, Sara Kate just lights in and starts eating. She doesn't ask any kind of a blessing for the food she's about to receive.

She dabbed at the corners of her mouth all dainty, like the women eating in fancy dining rooms in television movies. She raised her eyes and caught me staring at her. "Is there something wrong, Clover?" she asked.

It's funny how easy it's starting to get for me to tell Sara Kate exactly what's on my mind. "I was just wondering why you never, ever ask a blessing before you eat. Aunt Everleen says you should never stray away from the way you were raised up."

Sara Kate smiled. "In my family we never offered a blessing before meals, Clover."

I didn't say anything, but I thought to myself that was a mighty strange way to be raised up.

"Clover," she asked softly, "did Gaten offer prayer before meals?"

"Gaten wouldn't a bit more eat without saying a blessing, than he'd eat without washing his hands," I said.

"Does it make you unhappy that I don't ask a blessing?"

"No, I still say mine. Even if I do have to say it to myself."

Sara Kate laid down her fork and dabbed the corners of her mouth. I have to hand it to her, like Gaten, she eats really proper. There was a sad look in her eyes. "Clover," she said quietly, "I don't know how to say a blessing."

Someday I'm going to teach her how to ask the blessing. For sure I won't teach her one as long as Aunt Everleen's blessing. The food on the table gets cold sometimes before she finishes. She doesn't overlook a thing about the food. She gives thanks to the one who plants, weeds, gathers, cooks, and on and on.

Sara Kate hasn't asked me to teach her the blessing yet. But she will always ask me to say it before we eat. She always bows her head and closes her eyes. I know, because I always peep up at her every single time. I don't know if Sara Kate doesn't want to learn a blessing for fear she'll have to start calling on the Lord or what. One thing about her, she is not one bit religious.

I guess I'm going to have to hold all those things that happened here of late inside for awhile. Especially the spider thing. If Everleen knew that on account of what Sara Kate would have thought, I didn't kill a spider, she would declare I am natural-born crazy. Talk about having a doctor examine your head, she would hurry up and carry me to one.

It's Sunday again. The air outside is heavy with the smell of coffee and fried country ham. Inside, Sara Kate is still in her housecoat. She is drinking coffee and canned pineapple juice, and reading the Sunday *Charlotte Observer* newspaper.

Poor Gaten would have starved to death on what little cooking Sara Kate does. Sometimes I do wonder how she keeps on living. Everleen gave her a little peanut butter jar full of peach jelly and it looks like it's going to last her forever. She keeps it in the refrigerator and will stand there with the door open, eating one tiny teaspoonful. The jelly would go good on a hot butter biscuit. I have to give Daniel credit. Sara Kate is strange, strange.

I'm really hungry. I want to make me a bologna sandwich, but we don't have any white bread. There is no peanut butter. Sara Kate's spoon-eaten every bit of it. It's for sure I will have to go to my aunt's to get something good to eat.

I take the shortcut to Everleen's house. She's got to open up the peach shed at one o'clock, but she still had time to make a fresh peach cobbler for me and Sara Kate and one for her uncle Noah.

The crust on the cobbler was so juicy and good Sara Kate and I ate off the whole top. Now we have to get Everleen to put on a new crust. Gaten and I used to do it all the time.

I hate for Everleen to send me over to Noah's house on a Sunday. It was late one Sunday when he shot his sister that time. There was a boom, boom sound at his house. Then you could hear his sister screaming, and screaming like she was about to die. She was on the floor when we got there. Bright red blood was running from her hand onto the old worn wood floor.

As it turned out his sister didn't end up hurt all that bad. At the hospital they took out shotgun pellets from her hand, but missed one in her head, and gave her a tetanus shot and sent her back home. The next morning when she saw a group of her neighbors gathered in the road to talk about the shooting, she walked right down there and said all secretive-like, "Did you all hear about me getting shot last night? My fool brother shot me with his shotgun." Well, sir, all the snuff spit they'd been holding in their mouths flew right out. You could have knocked them over with a feather. She took all the gossip right out of their mouths. The woman should be on the stage.

There is not a one of Noah's old hound dogs in sight when I walk up on his porch. Maybe he's shot them, too. They say, when the crows cry caw, caw in the spring, Noah claims they are asking, "Is the corn ready?" So he gets his shotgun and tells them, "The corn is not ready. But my shotgun is."

Part of the porch is painted bright green. The other half is just old unpainted planks, gray with age. A step is broken half in two.

His sister is long gone now. Right after the shooting she took everything she owned to Gastonia, North Carolina. But she left the bloodstains behind. She never washed them up. She told her brother they would vanish at night like daylight swallowed up by the dark. "When the daylight comes," she'd warned, "they'll come back to haunt you for your sins." Everybody says it's the Lord's truth, too. You can see them stains as plain as your hand before your face. Noah has scrubbed and scrubbed, but he can't wash them out. The house smells like a chicken scalded in hot swamp water.

Through the screen door, I can see Noah

sitting near the window with his shotgun across his lap. Imagine fooling around with a gun on a Sunday.

Trouble sure can change a person. Noah used to be a right nice-looking man, his hair parted in the middle and all slicked down. And so much after-shave lotion and stuff, he smelled twice like a woman. Now he has turned into a picture of pained ugly. I think about the blood spots on the floor. A big family Bible on a table next to him is opened to a page with a picture on it. Cobwebs are everywhere. The room looks like it has been decorated for a Halloween party with spider's lace. An electric fan on the floor stirs dust balloons. They float all over the place. Maybe after all these years, Noah is trying to get saved. After the shooting he needs to do something.

I can hear his commode running. I need to go in and jiggle that handle. Gaten used to always check on stuff like that when he came over. Shucks, in the good old days I used to pick Noah's flowers in his yard, then sell them to him.

With Noah sitting there with his shotgun on his lap, I'm not about to touch that handle. I'm afraid to take the pie in and afraid to leave. I'm so scared, my hands are shaking.

Noah's mouth is stuck out like a twist clasp on a change purse. He cocks his shotgun when I drop the pie. I duck down and take off like a jack rabbit.

When I get to a patch of trees, I duck behind a bush and look back. Noah's old lazy hounds, Thunder and Lightning, are sneaking towards the pie. I think about the story of Epaminandos and how he stepped in his mother's pies. I don't turn back because I cannot bear to look.

Noah's sister's blood is still on that floor. A shotgun pellet still buried in her skull. And Everleen says Noah won't kill a dove. She claims the Lord's doing so much for Noah after they started praying for him at prayer meetings. "The Lord will help him," she said, "'cause Noah won't right in the head."

If Everleen wants to keep giving Noah stuff to eat she's going to have to take it herself. I'm not setting foot over there again.

I know what Everleen will end up saying. And it solid gets away with me when she does it. I can hear her now. "Now what would your daddy say, Clover?"

My father is dead, yet he speaks. Yes, even from the grave his hand reaches out to me. But not to comfort, only to correct.

Thirteen

♣ ♣ ♣

I can't figure out if Chase's daughter and niece came along to show off their new play shorts or to brag that they had been to camp. Those yellow and blue shorts are some kind of pretty. So is the girl in the yellow shorts.

"We went to camp last week," they whine through their noses at the same time. I'm not too crazy over the way Sara Kate talks, but it's way yonder better than theirs.

"I started to go to camp this summer," I say, "but I had to help sell my daddy's peaches. My daddy would have sat up in his coffin if we'd let all his peaches hit the ground. I went to Sweden, Norway, and Denmark last summer."

Sara Kate looked at me and drew quick breaths. Two, to be exact. Sucking in the same way she did when she thought I wasn't telling the truth when I said I didn't put the snake in her garden basket. I'm beginning to learn her better and better every day.

There is no way she can fool me now. She doesn't a bit more believe I've been to Norway and Denmark than a man in the moon. I can't see why she's getting so bent out of shape about three little towns somewhere down below Columbia. Grandpa said Norway was so little, you could spit clean across it.

The June bug I'd caught just before they drove up is digging its prickly legs into my hand. Sara Kate would die if she knew that I am planning to tie a string around the June bug's leg and make a helicopter. I guess I'd better turn it loose when she's not looking. I don't know why she got so upset over that old black snake. Looks like she'd have been glad I didn't kill him. Of course I didn't put that live snake in her basket. I won't let her know it, but I'm a little bit scared of snakes myself.

Yellow shorts whispers something to blue shorts. They giggle.

"I remember when you went, Clover," says Chase. "You told me if I lived there, I'd never stop shooting, because they have some kind of birds in Norway and Denmark."

Sara Kate's eyes are coming closer together. The green seems to darken. She's

201

not too hot on Chase killing birds. I sure don't know how she ended up marrying Gaten. He hunted all the time, and like Grandpa would shoot anything but a dove. Maybe she didn't know that about my daddy.

Anyway, Chase's kinfolks are having a cookout on the weekend and they are begging her to come. They don't say boo about me coming. Maybe it's because I look so bad. You see, Sara Kate fixed my hair. And that woman can't fix my kind of hair. I can't get it through her head that she can't set my hair when it's wet. My head looks like a puffed up fighting cock. They are looking at me like I'm a piece of moon rock or something. I really wish I were pretty.

My poor daddy. He always had a hard time with my hair. For years I had to ride the school bus, because my aunt messed over my hair too long to have me ready in time to ride with him. My hair would have still been a problem for Gaten. Because sure as there's a hell, Sara Kate couldn't fix it. After the peach season is over, Aunt Everleen is going to have a perm put in my hair.

Yellow shorts is telling Sara Kate about all the good stuff they are going to have at the cookout. "We are going to make two churns of homemade ice cream," she says.

"Please, please come, Sara Kate," blue shorts begs.

"I'm sorry, my dears," Sara Kate says in that smooth breathy voice of hers, "but I'm not sure yet what plans Clover may have made for us."

Chase grins his slow grin. "Clover, surely you wouldn't have anything planned that would be more fun for the two of you than the cookout?"

Sara Kate and I exchange looks. "It sounds like fun," I say. "Well, good," Sara Kate smiles, "then it's settled. We'll be delighted to come."

Yellow shorts and blue shorts are giggling and jumping up and down like a pair of hop-toads.

So we went to the cookout. I had a good time, but it sure isn't the way I want to spend the rest of my life. I got too many curious questioning stares when I walked about between the two of them with Sara Kate holding my hand.

Chase seemed to have been having a good time. I suppose he really was. Chase Porter happens to be a man who does whatever he wants and whenever. He said he doesn't give a damn what people say or think.

Come to think of it, maybe I didn't stand out so much after all. After a few weeks of sun Sara Kate could almost pass for one of us.

I guess it's the way she wanted to look. Even after she sloshed on a hundred different kinds of creams, moisturizers, anti-wrinkle cream, and sunscreen, she still added a suntan lotion. Seems to me the sun was enough. She spends so much money on stuff to block out the sun. Looks like if she didn't want the sun to hit her she wouldn't go out of her way to tan.

It's funny how the sun works. It may darken her skin but it sure takes the color out of her brown hair. It will be blonde if she's not careful.

It was barely getting dark when Chase drove us home from the cookout. I sat on the front steps waiting for Chase and Sara Kate to finish whatever it was that they were so seriously talking about. When they finally got out of the pickup they still stood talking at the edge of the yard.

I didn't hear Chase ask Sara Kate to marry him, nor the answer she gave him. All I know is in my presence she kissed him good-bye and said her decision not to marry him did not mean her caring for him had changed. "I think for now," she added, "loving each other is all Clover and I can handle."

Sara Kate made a pot of tea and poured a cup for each of us. She watched me dangle my legs from the kitchen stool.

"It's a good thing you were able to wear shorts to the cookout, Clover," she said. "You've outgrown practically everything. You will definitely need new school clothes. Maybe we should start shopping soon."

I think of all the money Sara Kate might spend on school stuff. "I hope you won't spend too much on new clothes," I say. "Like Grandpa always used to say, 'when push comes to shove you can always wash and wear the same clothes over and over again.'

"You see, Sara Kate," I blurt out, "if you really have the money for school clothes I'd rather you not buy so many and save some towards a purple ten-speed bicycle for me."

My wish, practically the only wish I've ever had in my whole life, just slid right out.

Sara Kate looked surprised. She smiled, "Why, Clover, if it's a ten-speed purple bicycle you want then that's what you'll get. But we'll still have to get some new school clothes."

I smile. In my mind I can see myself racing up and down the road, cruising down every path in Round Hill. My wish has finally come true. I am going to get my purple bicycle.

Fourteen

♣ ♣ ♣

When I look back and think about the way I treated Sara Kate that day at lunch, I can't help thinking, what in the world would Gaten have thought? I know one thing, I really hate I acted the way I did. I ran screaming and crying to my aunt Everleen like a little wild fool.

Maybe in the way things turned out, it all happened for the good. Because, you see, after that very day, Everleen and Sara Kate became closer. All because they were both siding with each other against me. I say that about them, but secretly I'm kind of glad that they both care enough about me to make me do the right thing. Maybe, when I am older, I will tell them that.

Sometimes, Sara Kate will pop in and out at the peach shed. When she takes a break from her "art work" as Daniel calls it, she will bring Tastee Freeze ice cream. Sometimes she brings ice tea with fresh mint leaves. Aunt Everleen drinks it, but not me.

If things had not changed between the two women, Sara Kate would have never been there, that hot August day. But there she was. Standing and chatting with Everleen in one of her skimpy halter tops, and the shortest shorts I'd ever seen. It was then that we heard a weak cry for help. It was coming from over in the Elberta peaches.

"It's Jim Ed," Everleen screamed. She started to run, but stopped and started running around and around in circles. She was going to pieces. "Go find help, Everleen, we'll find Jim Ed," Sara Kate screamed, as the two of us raced in the direction of his weak cries.

Poor Uncle Jim Ed lay under a peach tree with stinging yellow jackets swarming all over him. He had gotten his foot all tangled up in a trumpet vine and fell into the army of yellow jackets feeding on a pile of peaches someone had emptied out in the grass. There was doubtless a yellow jacket nest there on the ground also.

I guess once the stinging things got hold of Jim Ed and started stinging him like crazy, he couldn't help what he did. Like he didn't have a grain of sense, instead of trying to free himself so he could try to get away, he started fighting and killing the jokers. He knew better. He'd known all his life, if you kill one yellow jacket, two or more will come in to sting you. It seemed every yellow jacket there multiplied. They were everywhere. Jim Ed is allergic to any bee sting. You could almost see him swelling up. His eyes were already swollen closed.

Sara Kate didn't seem to think twice about the stinging bees. She plunged right into them and pulled Jim Ed out. The yellow jackets were soon all over her. She was getting stung like crazy. Yet she did not cry out in pain.

Jim Ed stopped gasping for breath. You could see he wasn't breathing. Sara Kate started crying, "Oh, no, Jim Ed, we can't lose you, too." She dropped to her knees, and while I fanned away yellow jackets with peach branch leaves, she gave Jim Ed mouth-to-mouth resuscitation.

A new red Ford pickup roared right through the peach orchard. In a split second, two men that I'd never seen before leaped out, put Jim Ed in the truck, and with Sara Kate at his side, sped away. I had to try and outrun the yellow jackets.

At the hospital, the doctors said after Sara

Kate had worked to revive him, they had gotten him there just in time. It was lucky she knew CPR.

Sara Kate had big welts all over her. She didn't swell up like Jim Ed, though. She is not as allergic to bee stings.

I think the people in Round Hill will talk about what she did for the rest of their lives.

Aunt Everleen has been having migraine headaches, one right after the other, ever since Uncle Jim Ed got stung. The big problem with her headache is, she forces you to have it along with her. My aunt does not like to suffer alone. So she tells you every pain she feels, everything she sees. I not only have to feel the throbbing pain that works its way up the back of her neck, pain that moves quickly across the top of her head to the eyes; I am also forced to see the flashing lights that dance a wild fire dance on her eyeballs. I do wish she wouldn't tell me about the people and things that sway and shimmer before her eyes like heat waves. It seems to make my eyes play tricks on me.

It's a good thing Sara Kate is helping her out until Uncle Jim Ed gets back. He doesn't seem in a rush to get better. I think he enjoys going over to the Bells and watching all the baseball games on cable TV. The Bells have a satellite dish in their front yard that's bigger than their house.

"If you can drive a stick shift, you can drive a tractor, Miss Sara Kate," said Gideon. He reached her a tractor key and showed her the gears. Sara Kate made only one mistake. She took the tractor out of gear when she stopped. Gideon stopped it from rolling into a gully.

I could have shown Sara Kate how to drive the tractor. Daniel could have, too. Nobody asked us, though.

Gideon has really put a fooling on Sara Kate. He has fooled her into paying him some money every day he's worked. "I just need a little piece of money to tide me over until tomorrow, Miss Sara Kate," he'd beg. Every day for awhile, Gideon would complain that he didn't have a lick of bread, lard, fatback, or something in his house. When Sara Kate gave him money, the next day he couldn't come to work. Or, if he did, he couldn't pick peaches.

I knew there was trouble the morning he staggered up, tipped his cap to a stack of peach baskets, and said, "Good morning. How are you feeling this fine morning?"

Gideon was hitting the bottle too hard to pick peaches.

Jim Ed knew better than to let him have money every day. He would just let him push his mouth into that ugly, juicy spout he always made, and get as mad as he wanted to. Sara Kate didn't know to do that.

Poor, poor Gideon. I guess he can't help himself. I will never forget when he was in that detox place, and Daniel and I didn't see Trixie, his little dog, anywhere. We knew Gideon would die if he came home and found out his dog was gone. So we went everywhere, calling "here Trixie, here Trixie." We searched even in the dark. Trixie was nowhere to be found.

"We looked everywhere for Trixie," we told Gideon when he came home, "but we couldn't find her. She must have run away." "Dogs will run off sometimes," was all Gideon said.

Later we found out that Gideon had sold Trixie for twenty dollars. He never said a word to us about what happened to his dog. One thing is for sure, he will never fool me again.

The swelling around Jim Ed's eyes is going down. You can finally see a little of his eyes peeping out through slits, like half-opened pea pods. One good thing, he can still see. Aunt Everleen took down the "Pick Your Own" sign. She is still burning up mad that it was some customer picking in the orchard who dumped the peaches on the ground where Jim Ed got stung. It was an awful thing for a person to do just because they happened upon a tree with bigger peaches. They had no right to pour out the ones they had. It made the act even worse when they happened to pick a tree that had yellow jacket nests under it.

I believe Everleen and Sara Kate are going to become friends. Everleen has started bragging about her a little bit. My sister-in-law did such and such, she'll say. Sara Kate takes up for her. Like with the golf thing. One day, Everleen sort of over-talked herself and led a fine lawyer to think she knew golf inside and out. Trapped, she was ashamed to admit she didn't play. She doesn't even know which end of a golf club to hit the ball with. So when the handsome lawyer asked her what her handicap was, she had no idea what he was talking about. She sort of crossed her eyes and cast her what-on-earth-are-you-talking-about look. She looked down, and said real soft like, "I guess my handicap is my old arthritic left knee." Everybody except Everleen started to laugh, but when Sara Kate hurriedly said, "Everleen has a great sense of humor, and such a sharp, keen wit," then Everleen laughed, too.

After Jim Ed came back to the peach shed, Gideon straightened up and has been in the peach orchard every morning. Even things at home are going good. People are starting to drop by. People other than Jim Ed and Everleen. After the yellow jacket thing, they walk over almost every evening after we close the peach shed. They sit out under the big oaks in the front yard and talk until dark.

Gaten's hammock is still stretched between two of the trees. Sometimes Jim Ed will rest there until it's time to go home. It's almost like old times.